Fly Away

 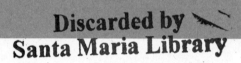

Fly Away

Nora Rock

orca sports

ORCA BOOK PUBLISHERS

Library and Archives Canada Cataloguing in Publication

Rock, Nora, 1968-
Fly away / written by Nora Rock.
(Orca sports)

Also issued in an electronic format.
ISBN 978-1-55469-341-2 (bound).--ISBN 978-1-55469-313-9 (pbk.)

I. Title. II. Series: Orca sports
PS8635.O32F59 2010   jC813'.6   C2010-903538-0

First published in the United States, 2010
Library of Congress Control Number: 2010928827

Summary: Marnie is forced into a leadership role on her
competitive cheerleading team, but it's harder than she imagined to keep
the Soar Starlings—and herself—aloft.

Mixed Sources
Cert no. SW-COC-001271
© 1996 FSC
FSC

*Orca Book Publishers is dedicated to preserving the environment and has printed
this book on paper certified by the Forest Stewardship Council.*

Orca Book Publishers gratefully acknowledges the support for its publishing
programs provided by the following agencies: the Government of Canada
through the Canada Book Fund and the Canada Council for the Arts, and the
Province of British Columbia through the BC Arts Council and
the Book Publishing Tax Credit.

Typesetting by Nadja Penaluna
Cover photography by Getty Images
Author photo by Chuck Shumilak

ORCA BOOK PUBLISHERS
PO Box 5626, Stn. B
Victoria, BC Canada
v8R 6s4

ORCA BOOK PUBLISHERS
PO Box 468
Custer, WA USA
98240-0468

www.orcabook.com
Printed and bound in Canada.

13 12 11 10 • 4 3 2 1

For Marley

chapter one

When the paramedics came charging into Soar's gym, every one of us stared at the same thing: their boots. Both of them—the woman and the man—wore heavy rubber-soled work boots that shed chunks of gray slush on the crash mats. If we have one rule at Soar, it's no outdoor shoes on the mats. Seeing the paramedics run across the mats like that, with Coach Saylor waving them on, seemed to drive the message home: we'd witnessed a very serious accident.

1

With the rescue team on the scene and Emma's curled-up body blocked from view, I suddenly realized that my legs were shaking violently. Just as I was about to lose my balance, a steady hand grasped my forearm.

"Whoa, girl," whispered Arielle, guiding me to the floor. "You okay?"

I nodded. The trembling had migrated upward to my shoulders, and now my teeth were chattering too. Arielle sat down beside me and draped one arm across my shoulders. We sat like that, in silence, while the paramedics eased Emma onto the stretcher and strapped her in. The woman paramedic was talking with Coach Saylor. I couldn't make out what was being said because of the ringing in my ears.

The paramedic looked at me and said something. I opened my mouth to speak, but I couldn't make my jaw work.

"I think she's just in shock," said Arielle. "You're not hurt, are you?"

I shook my head, thinking back to the accident. I remembered Emma's body twisting in midair as she tried to avoid the base girl on her left. She was too far over for me to do anything to break her fall. I had reached for her and missed. Her shoulder dropped awkwardly toward the mat, hitting it with a sickening crunch.

The paramedic gave me a quick once-over anyway, checking my pulse and looking into my eyes with a penlight. "She seems fine."

Arielle nodded. "I'll keep an eye on her."

The other girls, who'd been whispering nervously while Emma was carried out, were beginning to gather around us.

Coach Saylor had a hand up, trying to get our attention. "Girls!" she said. "Gather round. Sit down. Shona, Janelle, never mind the slush. Sit down, please."

The rest of my team—the Soar Starlings All-Star Cheerleaders, senior level five—obeyed. I could tell that some of them, like me, were grateful to get off shaky legs.

"Girls, we're done for today. I know you're scared. But Emma's in good hands. She's on her way to the hospital. Her father will meet her there."

Arielle shifted beside me so that she could put her free arm across Priya's shoulders. Priya was the rear spotter in Emma's stunt group, the girl who boosts the flyer into the basket and then up into the air for aerial stunts. Emma had been hurt doing a back tuck. Like a backward somersault, but in midair. It's one of the toughest throw moves, but Emma had done it dozens of times before.

"You all know," continued Coach Saylor, "that cheerleading is a dangerous sport. You Starlings are the most experienced team in this club. But no amount of experience can prevent all accidents. What happened to Emma"—Coach Saylor looked in turn at Priya, Amy Jo and Jada, the bases in Emma's stunt group—"was nobody's fault. I want you to understand that. And now, I want you to shower up, go home, and get a good night's sleep. If I hear any news about

Emma's condition, I'll post it on the team's Facebook page. If you need to talk, don't hesitate to call Arielle. Or call me at home. You understand?"

Thirteen ponytails bobbed in unison.

"Good," said Coach.

I stood up, steadier now. I felt okay. I turned to tell Arielle I was feeling better, but she was busy comforting Priya, who had burst into tears.

"But my hand slipped off her leg," Priya said. "And I couldn't–"

"Shh!" said Arielle. "You heard the coach. It wasn't your fault."

"But..."

Arielle hugged Priya to calm her down. Over Priya's back, she gave me a questioning look. I mimed shampooing my hair and pointed to the locker room. Arielle nodded.

Arielle was our team captain and my best friend. This was her third and final year as a Starling. She'd be turning nineteen in January, which would make her too old to qualify as a senior for the spring championships. Arielle has been cheer-leading since our club, Soar, opened, when she was eight years old. She's exactly the kind of girl you imagine when you think "cheerleader." She has straight honey-blond hair and long graceful limbs, and she's never in a bad mood. As our captain, she has to deal with thirteen other teenage girls' stresses and tantrums and complaints. She does it with a smile on her face. Some people think cheerleaders are ditzy and that our sport is not a true team sport. Those people have not met Arielle Kuypers.

I took a quick shower, feeling jittery and distracted. The locker room was buzzing with theories about Emma's condition. A few of the girls were insisting that she'd cracked her skull. "What else would make her pass out like that?" reasoned Shona. But Amy Jo, who'd been the closest to Emma when she landed, insisted that she hadn't fallen on her head. I stayed out of it.

I'd gotten a ride with Arielle, so, as usual, we were the last to leave. We shuffled quickly across the parking lot in a bitter January wind. I turned the heater on full blast when we got in Arielle's car.

She turned to me before pulling out. "Want to sleep over at my place tonight? You still seem kind of shaky."

"I'm fine," I told her. "Besides, it's Monday."

"Ah, yes," she said. "Geek night."

chapter two

Geek night is the night that my boyfriend Liam and I go to his cousin Eliza's house to play Blood Plain. Blood Plain is a role-playing game, sort of like Dungeons and Dragons, but with North American Indians. My character is a Sioux squaw named Chumani.

The game is really fun, and Liam's cousin's friends are cool. Most of them go to the University of Guelph, so they're a little older than me and Liam, but they don't talk down to us. I think Eliza's just happy to have another girl there.

I was looking forward to going. I knew that if I stayed home, I'd sit around replaying Emma's accident over and over in my head and working myself up into a panic. But before we reached my house, I got a text from Liam saying he couldn't go.

"Why not?" Arielle asked.

I shrugged. "He doesn't say." It was the second time he'd bailed on geek night that month.

"Then you're staying at my place after all," said Arielle.

We stopped at my house to leave a note for my mom. I stuffed some clothes in an overnight bag, and we headed for Arielle's house.

She lives in the coolest house I've ever seen. It's supermodern, made up of lots of cubes. Arielle has a cube all to herself, with a bedroom, bathroom, art studio and its own entrance. I walked in ahead of her and gasped.

"You finished it!"

Arielle smiled. "Surprise!"

In the middle of the room was Arielle's latest painting. It was on a canvas as big as three refrigerators side by side. She'd painted people at a carnival, but not the way you'd paint them if someone told you to paint people at a carnival. It was so close-up that the people were life-size, most of them too tall to fit completely in the frame. Their backs were turned to the viewer, and they were watching something ahead of them. The only person whose face you could see was a little girl. She was half-turned, looking straight out of the canvas with terror in her eyes. I shuddered.

"What do you think?" Arielle asked.

I put my hands over my face. "It gives me the creeps!"

Arielle laughed. "It's supposed to."

"It's really good," I said. "It makes me feel guilty just looking at it. Like I'm a kidnapper about to grab her."

Arielle smiled happily and leaned the canvas against the wall with two others.

All of Arielle's paintings made you feel like you were missing something that lay just beyond the borders of the image.

"It's your best ever," I added.

"Thanks, Mar," she said, tossing her cheerleading duffel into the corner.

We headed to the kitchen to make some supper. It was late, and Arielle's parents had already eaten. Arielle checked her phone to see if there was a call from Coach Saylor or from Emma's dad, but there was nothing.

"So," she said when we'd carried our grilled cheese sandwiches to the couch, "what's the deal with Liam?"

I thought about pretending I didn't know what she was talking about. But Arielle was my best friend. If there was anyone I could be open with, it was her. "I don't know what's going on," I said softly. "That's what scares me. He's never kept anything from me before." Liam and I had been dating for more than two years, since the summer before ninth grade, when he was about to turn sixteen.

"You've tried to get him to talk?"

"I've tried everything. He says there's nothing wrong. But it's like he's a whole different person." I bit my bottom lip to stop it from quivering.

"I'm sorry to be such a baby," I said. "I'm just a little shaken up."

"Me too," Arielle said.

"What about Priya?" I asked. "How do you think she's doing?"

"It wasn't Priya's fault, Marnie. Accidents happen. The whole group's timing was off. Emma didn't get enough height for the tuck. I'm sure she doesn't blame Priya."

What Arielle said was true. No one girl can make or break a stunt on her own. The thrown back tuck is one of the hardest stunts we do. It takes perfectly timed cooperation.

I took a deep breath, forced a smile and changed the subject. "So, you've been pretty intense with your painting lately. You still chatting with that guy online?" Arielle belonged to an online artists' community. Even though she was still in high school, her work was starting to get some serious notice.

Arielle nodded. "He's been so fantastic, Marnie. He's been telling me exactly what I need to do to move my career along."

"By not doing any shows?" I asked. Arielle had been invited to be part of an exhibition at a local art gallery, but she'd pulled out at the last minute. It didn't make a lot of sense to me.

She laughed. "I'm not quite ready. Besides," she added, "what does it matter to you? You see my paintings all the time. You must be sick to death of my stuff by now."

I shook my head. "Impossible. You're the best artist I know."

Arielle smiled. "More like the only artist you know."

chapter three

Coach Saylor called while we were making up the daybed for me in Arielle's room. Emma had just come out of surgery to fix a compound collarbone fracture. She was doing fine and had no head injury. She was also out of cheerleading for the rest of the season.

I was so relieved. I had been afraid it was something much worse, especially since Emma had been unconscious.

But Coach Saylor told Arielle that sometimes pain makes people pass out.

This was supposed to be our big year. We'd placed second at the provincials the previous two years, and we were better than ever. While nobody came out and said it, we all felt like it was our turn to win it all. I could imagine how Emma was feeling about being out for the season. Emma is low-key and not outwardly competitive, but you never really know what's going on in someone's head. I bet she was pretty bummed.

Nobody, not even Arielle, knew how badly I had wanted to take Sophia Damonte's place as a flyer when she moved away last summer. Shona Bart was promoted instead, from level three. She's really good, so I said nothing. Coach Saylor reminded me I was more valuable as a tumbler and that good tumblers are harder to find than good flyers. I understood, but I was really disappointed. Now here I was, wanting Emma's spot before she'd even been released from hospital. I tried to force the thought out of my head. I had to get some sleep.

Sure enough, I was tired and cranky the next day, and the school day seemed to crawl by. It was mid-January and bitterly cold, the kind of weather that makes me feel sluggish and antisocial. I knew, though, that I needed to talk to Liam. Since when could he cancel plans at the last minute and with no reason? I tracked him down in the cafeteria and stood behind his chair.

Liam and I have rules about lunchtime. We eat lunch together Mondays and Thursdays only. We decided a long time ago that we didn't want to be one of those couples that spend their high-school years stuck together like glue. You can miss out on a lot if you do that.

Liam was sitting with some of his jock buddies. He plays football, and he's on the wrestling team, so he's friendly with a bunch of those guys. Liam sat a little apart from the group, with his head down. He was staring into his chili like it was some kind of science experiment. I put my hand on his shoulder.

He turned around. "Hey, Mar."

"I know it's not Thursday," I said, "but we need to talk."

I pushed his untouched chili aside and perched on the table, my back to the other guys.

"What's up?" Liam asked. He didn't seem annoyed that I was bugging him on one of our "off" days, but he didn't seem happy to see me either. He just seemed...blank.

"That was the second time in a row you ditched geek night."

He shrugged, almost in slow motion. If I hadn't known better, I would have worried that he was high. But Liam's not like that.

"I had a headache," he said.

"A bad one?" Maybe he was sick. Maybe he had mono or something.

"A regular headache. No biggie." He looked at me balefully, his big brown eyes full of annoyance.

"Well then," I said, "you should have taken a Tylenol and made it out to Eliza's."

"Chill out, Mar," he growled.

I hopped down off the table in disgust.

"Hey," said the guy across the table from Liam, "you gonna eat this chili?"

Liam shook his head, pushed the chili toward his friend and turned back to me. "You have cheerleading tomorrow?"

I nodded.

"What about Thursday? You free on Thursday night?"

"Yeah," I said.

"Then let's do something on Thursday night. Okay?" He reached over and squeezed my arm, his palm warm on my skin.

As I walked away, I realized I hadn't told him about Emma's accident. And he hadn't even asked me how I was.

On Wednesday, when we got to practice, a new girl was there. She had red hair cut in a cute bob. A couple of the younger girls gave her a welcoming hug. She'd been promoted from level three, so they had all been teammates before they became Starlings. Coach Saylor sure hadn't wasted any time replacing Emma.

"Girls," Coach Saylor said after we gathered on the mats, "as you all know, Emma is recovering from surgery. She was discharged from hospital this morning, and her dad tells me she's doing fine. Arielle bought her a gift from the team"— Coach gestured toward a gift bag sitting on a table in the corner—"so you'll all need to chip in."

Most of the girls turned to look at the gift bag, and I took the opportunity to check out the new girl. She was a couple of inches taller than me. Maybe fifty kilos. Inconclusive. Flyers tend to be small, but not always. The new girl wasn't too big to be a flyer.

"Please sign the card at the end of practice," Coach Saylor said. Then she beckoned for the new girl to come forward.

"Girls, this is Lucy O'Reilly. She has agreed to join our team while Emma recovers. Some of you know her from the level-three Cardinals, where she's been a base girl for the past two years."

Base girl. Base girl. I wondered if anyone else could hear my heart. It was thumping so loud, I thought it would burst out of my chest. Was it possible?

The other girls were clapping. I joined in, flashing Lucy a big smile.

"And since Lucy is a base," Coach said, "we now have to replace the flyer in Emma's group."

I couldn't look at Coach Saylor. I was too nervous. I stared at Lucy instead. I waited for Coach to say, "Marnie, we really need you as a tumbler..."

Instead I heard her say, "And I can't think of a better girl for the job of flyer than our own Marnie Goodwood."

chapter four

The moment we were in Arielle's car and out of earshot of the team, I pounced.

"Did you know?"

She smiled sideways at me. "I really expected you to hound me about it, Marnie! Way to keep your cool."

I laughed. Self-control is not exactly my strong suit. "Well, I didn't want to disrespect Emma. And I knew you'd never tell me what Coach was planning. You're always so professional. But I'm superexcited!" It had been more than an hour since the coach's announcement, and I still had butterflies in my stomach.

Arielle turned the key in the ignition. "You earned it."

Something in her voice made me pull myself together. I wondered about Arielle's own feelings. "Did you ever want to be a flyer?"

"If I ever did," she said, "it was so long ago that I don't remember. I'm way too tall anyway."

As we pulled out of the parking lot, I wondered how anyone could forget something like that.

I was awake half that night, still hyper from the big news. The next day, the best I could do was coast foggily through the school day. I knew that if I had any hope of getting into the University of Toronto—where Arielle was going in September—I had to pay attention and get my marks up this year and next. But an off day here or there wouldn't kill me, I reasoned. Except that I was headed for a second late night in a row. Liam had agreed to come with me that night to a party at Ashleigh's. Ashleigh was a cheerleader who lived in Tavistock, a smaller town just east of ours.

When I reminded Liam after school, he groaned and said, "Not tonight, Marnie."

"But you said you would come!" I said.

If he didn't drive, I'd have to find another way to get there. "Okay, Marnie," he said, as if he was doing me a huge favor. "I'll go."

It was a party. As in, a little bit of fun for a change. Sheesh.

Liam and I had pizza at his place before the party. When it was nine thirty and time for us to head out, he balked. He tried to convince me that we were having fun already. We'd played video games until I got frustrated with losing, and then we'd watched a stupid movie. He wanted to start another one. Never mind even trying to get me to go downstairs, where we could make out. He just wanted to sit and stare at the screen.

"But I said I'd go," I said.

"Just call Ashleigh and tell her you're worried about the roads. It's January."

"The roads are clear, Liam. It hasn't snowed in a week. We only need to stay for a couple of hours..."

"Fine," he said. "I'll drop you off."

What kind of boyfriend does that? "It's not like you have anything better to do!" I said.

"I'm just not in the mood," he said.

I played my last card. "I made flyer. Finally, after two years of waiting. Don't you think that's worth celebrating?"

He pulled himself to his feet. "It's not a party for you, Marnie. You're just trying to talk me into going."

He walked to the hall closet to get his coat with all the enthusiasm of a person walking into a dentist's office. I followed in a funk. If he dropped me off, how would I get home?

"You know what?" I said. "Don't even bother. I wouldn't want to put you out."

I grabbed my coat and walked out the door. Once I was around the corner, I called Arielle on my cell phone.

"Hey," she said. "Where you calling from?"

"A snowbank," I told her. "I just walked out on Liam. Are you at Ashleigh's yet?"

She told me she was partway there, but that she'd turn around to get me. That's what real friends do.

By the time she arrived, I was shivering. I climbed into the backseat. Lucy O'Reilly, Emma's replacement, was riding shotgun. That was so like Arielle, being sure to include the new girl. I'd known Arielle long enough not to be jealous. I sank into the warm upholstery and sighed.

"So, what happened?" Arielle asked.

"He was supposed to come. He bailed at the last minute. So I blew him off."

"I'm sorry, Mar."

"No biggie," I answered. "I don't need him there. He'll just bring me down."

"Marnie's boyfriend," Arielle explained to Lucy, "is, um, kinda moody these days."

Except, I thought, he never used to be. Not until this year.

I had so much fun at that party. I love Liam, but it was a nice change not having to pay attention to whether or not he was having a good time. He can be hard to please. He doesn't like it when I get too hyper, and he never seems happy around my cheerleader friends.

"Do you have a boyfriend, Arielle?" Lucy asked on the ride home.

Arielle shook her head. "Nobody can stand me for more than two or three dates."

"But you're so gorgeous!" Lucy exclaimed.

Arielle laughed. I knew her well enough to know that making the effort to hang on to a boyfriend had never been a priority for her. She made time for her studies, her cheerleading and her painting. Everything else took a backseat. If there was a guy out there independent enough to keep up with her, she hadn't met him yet.

"Listen, Lucy," said Arielle, "do you think you could make it to the gym on Saturday for a couple of hours to help Marnie work on her stunts? She was a flyer when she was level three, but that was a couple of years ago. I'm sure she'd appreciate the practice."

"Sure," said Lucy. "No problem. I'd love to."

"I'll call Priya," Arielle promised. "Then we'll have three bases. We could meet at Soar at eleven."

That practice session didn't go so well.

Maybe it was because Lucy was new and she wasn't used to Priya's and Arielle's lifting rhythm. Maybe it was just me. I was popping up fine. I'm short and only 103 pounds, so I'm easy to lift. But once I was up, I was shaky. My ankles wouldn't stop wobbling, so every throw was off-kilter.

After a while the girls' arms were aching, and I was a little heap of misery and shame. I sat on the floor, pulled my knees up to my face and hid behind my thick bangs.

Priya and Lucy sat on either side of me.

"Hel-lo," Arielle said. "Come out from behind the hair."

They waited. I sulked.

Arielle lifted my bangs away from my face. "Coach Saylor used to hate this hair," she told the other two girls. "She wondered how Marnie could see through it. So one day, she made her tuck her bangs under a headband."

"Made me look like an alien," I mumbled, my head still buried in my knees.

Arielle nodded. "She did look strange. Half the squad ran away. And that was the end of the headband experiment."

Priya and Lucy giggled.

"I suck," I whimpered, "and I'm an extra-terrestrial."

"Well, you've had better practices, Mar. But aren't you glad you got the kinks out in front of us instead of the whole team?"

I sniffled.

"Why don't we forget about the throws for today? Work on scorpion and liberty. Okay?"

"And if you don't mind," Lucy piped up, "I could really use a couple of run-throughs of the drill parts in the seventies routine."

I'd been so wrapped up in my own poor performance that I'd forgotten how new our choreography was to Lucy. "Let's do that first, then," I suggested, getting to my feet. "Take my mind off the stunts for a bit."

Arielle found our music, and we lined up in front of the mirror. Drill is the part of cheerleading that's sort of like dance— the part where you keep your feet on the floor and interpret the music. There's a lot of pressure, in competition, to do stunt after stunt. Some people even say drill cheerleading is dying and that in a couple of years it'll be extinct, like the pom-pom. But our coach always tells us that drill is the element that separates the good squads from the bad. If a team has a weak link or two, you can hide it on stunts—after all, how much grace does it take to hold up a leg? But when you watch a team do drill, your eye is drawn, like a magnet, to the girl who's half a beat too slow, or whose toes aren't pointed. Strong drill is a hallmark of our team.

Twenty minutes of drill left all of us sweaty and breathing hard. It's hard to be nervous when you're tired. When Arielle reminded me we still hadn't worked on the lifts, I lined up in front of the three bases without objection.

"One, two," recited Arielle.

I lifted my foot off the ground for the boost.

"Three, four," answered Lucy and Priya, bending their knees and taking hold of my left foot and right ankle.

"Five, six," I said, pushing off the bases' shoulders on five and raising my arms above my head on six.

For "seven, eight"—which we count in our heads—I'm more than six feet above the ground, supported only by three palms under the sole of my right foot and one hand around my ankle. My left toe is pointed against my right knee, and my arms are in the air. The only thing that keeps me from falling in a liberty lift is the strength of my stomach muscles and how rigid and straight I keep my ankle and my knee. Any wobble anywhere, and the whole thing comes crashing down in a heap.

"Down," whispered Arielle, and the web of palms below my foot collapsed, forming a basket to break my fall.

"Nice," said Lucy, setting me down on my feet.

"Well," I protested, "I kept my hands on your shoulders too long, but—"

"No," said Arielle, "that was nice. Now, let's do a scorpion."

chapter five

I was nervous during Monday's warm-up. Saturday's fiasco had proved that, even though my lifts were coming along, my flying skills were seriously rusty. I stayed quiet while we stretched, trying to focus on the task ahead.

I was new at flying, at least on this level-five team. I was well liked, so the girls would probably cut me some slack, but only for so long. After all, this was supposed to be our breakout year. Second place wasn't going to cut it. I had only a few weeks to go from crummy to perfect.

"Let's go," said Coach.

We practiced the drill sequence first—the part that comes right after the opening stunts. Because it's on the floor, my part didn't change much. I just moved one row back to make way for Jada, who was taking my place as a tumbler.

When it comes to drill, timing and precision are key. Precision comes from positioning. Arms tight and straight, abdominal muscles taut, toes pointed. Each position must be held crisply, never drifted through.

Great music helps. Since I was friends with Arielle, I got to help choose our music, and I loved it. Many teams just pick whatever's popular at the moment, to please the crowd. This time we decided to go retro. One of our routines was a medley of seventies songs, from Led Zeppelin right through to disco. We called the routine "Groovy."

Working on drill helped settle me down. By the time we moved on to stunts, I felt competent. There are three stunt groups.

Arielle was on the other side of the room with her group. Lucy, who's in my group, shot me a nervous little smile as we got into position for the first lift. She was new too, I reminded myself. If we wobbled a little, it would be perfectly normal.

But we wobbled a lot. And Lucy wasn't the problem.

After I bailed out of a basic split throw for the second time, Shona Bart, the flyer from the center group, turned and stared at me. "What's wrong with you?" she demanded.

"Huh?"

"This is, like, a level-two throw. What's the matter?"

A hot blush crept up my neck.

"She hasn't done this in two years," Priya retorted. "She's just rusty. And Lucy just joined us."

Shona turned her back to me and said something to Ruthie that ended in "...get her act together in time for provincials." That didn't make me feel any steadier.

"What was that all about?" I complained when Arielle and I got into her car.

"You mean Shona?" Ari asked. "You know what she's like."

Anyone who's ever done a "girl sport"— figure skating, gymnastics, whatever—has met a girl like Shona Bart. The type who thinks a little talent gives her the right to criticize girls who've been doing the sport longer. That was what bugged me the most. Shona was only fourteen—she looked about nine—and I was sixteen.

"Yeah, well," I continued, "the problem is, she's right. I can't even do a stupid split throw! What's wrong with me?" I put my hands over my face.

Arielle laughed.

"Oh, nice," I said. "Laughing makes it so much better."

She shrugged. "Nothing's wrong, Marnie. You're rusty. Sometimes Shona flubs throws too, you know."

"When?" I asked. "When was the last time you saw Shona miss a throw?" Shona was a dependable performer. Rock solid.

"If you want," said Arielle, "I could sabotage her. Bump one of her bases at exactly the right moment…"

I wasn't sure I liked Ari making a joke out of my problems. But maybe I really did need to shake it off. Maybe I was being self-centered. Arielle was a very good listener. It's easy to dump on her and forget that she might need to talk about her own stuff too.

"So what's new with you, Ari?" I asked. "Any decisions about residence?" Arielle still hadn't made up her mind where she wanted to live at U of T.

She shrugged. "I guess Woodsworth. Unless I like the Lorretto house better when I take the tour."

"Isn't Lorretto girls-only?" I stuck out my tongue. "Bleah. When do you go for the tour? Want me to come?" We were hoping to live together when I got to U of T. Assuming I got accepted.

"Sure," she said. "Remind me to find some time to go."

"You don't seem too excited."

She shrugged again. "It's months away."

I wondered if having to leave cheerleading was one of the reasons she wasn't
excited. But Arielle hardly ever talked about
herself, and I didn't want to pry. Would
I miss cheerleading too when it was time
for me to go to Toronto?

"So, Liam canceled geek night again,"
I told her. "He's mad at me for walking out
on him before that party. Want to get
together and watch last year's DVD from the
provincials? Scope out the competition?"

But she told me she couldn't, that she
had stuff to do. Then she dropped me off
at my house.

I wondered what "stuff" Arielle was doing
on a Monday night. Probably painting. I
sat alone on my bed for about ten minutes.
What was I going to do? There was a social
studies essay I could start. I could try to
talk my mom into watching the provincials
DVD with me, but it wasn't as though she'd
have much to say about it. My mom always
likes to tell me she was a science nerd in

high school. She doesn't come right out and say that she thinks cheerleading is a waste of time, but she rarely has the energy to fake much interest in it. It's just too girlie for her.

I picked up the phone. Might as well see if I could patch things up with Liam.

His mother answered. "Marnie!" she chirped. "You haven't been over in ages."

She hadn't been home when I'd been at Liam's on Thursday, but I didn't want to argue. "Yeah." I said. "I guess it's a busy time of year."

"Really? I feel like Liam never leaves the house these days. I guess football's over, and..." Her voice trailed off. "Aren't you two supposed to be at Eliza's tonight? Playing that game?"

I heard Liam in the background. "Mom! Gimme the phone."

"Liam wants the phone," she said. "Come over soon, okay, honey?"

"I will," I promised.

"So," Liam said.

"We're gonna get kicked out of Blood Plain, you know," I said, "if we never show up."

"Whatever."

"Nice."

"Look, Marnie," he said, "I'm tired. If you feel the need to give me grief, it's going to have to wait."

"Until when?"

There was a long pause. "Tomorrow. We can get together tomorrow. It's cheap night at the movies. Work for you?"

I didn't seem to have much choice.

chapter six

The next morning I turned on my computer to print my social studies notes. There were no email messages from Liam, but there was one message pending, something that was taking forever to load. With my luck, it was a computer virus. I left it loading while I dried my hair. When I came back, I saw it was a note from Arielle, with several attachments. I opened it.

Hey Mar!

Can you take a look at this stuff? It's a portfolio of my recent stuff. It took me forever to get the images all the same size. But mostly I want you to look at the bio, see if it's okay. I want to sound like a serious artist without coming across like I'm full of myself...

Check it out and write back ASAP!

Ari

I checked the time of her email. 2:49 AM. So this was the "stuff" she had been so eager to work on. She must have stayed up half the night doing it. I reread the email to see who she was sending the portfolio to.

She didn't say.

I checked my watch. Ten minutes before I had to leave. I sat down to look at the images.

The first one was the carnival painting that she'd finished the previous week. I didn't recognize some of the other images. One in particular caught my eye. It was a painting of a guy on a skateboard, shoulders hunched, chin tucked into his jacket collar, hurrying away from something. He was looking down—you could barely see the side of his face—but you could tell by his posture that he was afraid. I shuddered. Arielle's work was getting creepier. But it seemed to me that it was also getting really good.

The bio Arielle had written seemed okay to me. She made no mention of cheerleading or the debate team or any of the other things she did so well. It was all about her art. The courses she'd taken. The shows she's been in. It seemed like she was trying to sound older than she was, more mature. Maybe she had to do that to be taken seriously.

I dialed her number on the way to school.

She answered right away. "Did you get my message?"

"Yep. The skateboarder painting is amazing."

"That's my cousin Doug," she said. "He posed for it."

"Was he being chased by zombies at the time?"

She laughed. "Did you read the bio though? I'm worried it seems sort of...brief."

"You're eighteen. What do they expect?" It was freezing out. I pulled my hood tighter around my face. "Who's this portfolio for anyway?"

"Oh, well," she said, "you know. Nobody in particular. It's good to have something prepared so I can send it if anyone asks, right?"

"I guess," I said. Who stays up until 2:00 AM to prepare something just in case?

I knew that Arielle had wanted to study fine arts at university, but her parents convinced her that a Bachelor of Science was the way to go. She gets great marks in science. There was no reason why she couldn't keep painting, arts program or not. But Ari had seemed disappointed.

43

Was she planning to apply to the fine arts program after all? Her parents would freak. And the deadline had to be soon, if it hadn't passed already. But why wasn't she talking to me about it? What was wrong with everybody these days?

My bad mood lasted the rest of the day. I kept quiet, riding next to Liam on the way to the movies. If he could be moody, then so could I.

But the movie was really funny, and it was so good to hear Liam laugh. He's really the sweetest guy when he's not depressed. He almost always made time for me when I needed it. And he's so cute. He has the biggest, brownest eyes you've ever seen, like melted chocolate. I squeezed his hand in the darkness.

"What?"

"Nothing," I whispered.

He squeezed my hand back.

We took the long way home and parked in the empty golf course lot. We got out to look at the stars. It was one of those windless midwinter nights, when it seems like you can see the whole Milky Way. We stood there for a long time, his arms wrapped around me.

"This cheerleading stuff, Marnie, it's all going to be fine. You know that, right?"

I nodded.

"It's your year," he said. "And it's going to happen just like you want it to happen."

I could tell, when he said that, that it wasn't really me he was thinking about. About a month ago, Liam had finally realized that the football scholarship he'd been counting on wasn't coming through. When he said good things were going to happen for me, I knew he couldn't say the same thing about himself. I squeezed his hand. Poor Liam. No wonder he'd been so down lately. But I didn't say anything about it. We'd had such a nice night together. I couldn't bring myself to wreck it.

chapter seven

Emma visited us at practice on Monday. Everyone was so happy to see her. Her left arm was stuck in a funny position, supported by a steel post, and her whole shoulder was encased in plaster. The girls swarmed around her, asking questions.

"How can you sleep with that thing on?"

"Does it hurt?"

"Does it itch?"

"When does it come off?"

Emma laughed, accepting hug after hug with her good arm. She explained that her shoulder hadn't hurt much since the surgery, but that sleeping was tough, and her hand was always freezing from being up in the air like that. She congratulated me on making flyer.

I squeezed her good hand. "You'll be back soon, Emma. Don't worry. You are coming back, right?"

She nodded. "Of course. But not until, like, September or something."

"Do we ever miss you," said Shona pointedly.

I knew the comment was not really meant for Emma, but for me.

I didn't say anything, but when we split up into our stunt groups, I was determined to prove Shona wrong. "Let's practice that split throw," I said to Priya.

"Are you sure?" she said. It was the throw I'd had so much trouble with at the previous practice.

"Of course, I'm sure," I said, trying to hide the fact that I didn't feel sure at all.

47

"I've been thinking about what might be going wrong. Could you try throwing me not quite so high? Then I won't have as much time to wobble. Once I'm steady, we'll work on height."

Lucy shrugged. "Worth a try."

For the first time that month, Liam and I actually made it to geek night. Eliza and the others were cool about our missed sessions.

"Just so you know," I warned, "I have to miss another night. Two weeks from now."

"Oh yeah?" Eliza asked. "Where are you going?"

"Toronto," I told her. "With my cheerleading team. We're going to the Great Lakes Championship."

"What sport?" asked Dave, one of the guys I didn't know very well.

"Cheerleading," I repeated.

"Yeah, but for what? Basketball? Football?"

I shook my head. "Not cheering for a team. We're competing. Cheerleading is an independent sport, you know. It's like gymnastics and dance, all in one."

"Dance is not a sport," Dave said.

"Can you hold your right foot over your head with one hand, while your left foot is six feet above the ground, balanced on somebody's palm?" I asked.

Dave frowned, trying to picture a scorpion lift in his head.

"Well," I said, "once you've mastered that stunt, we should chat about whether or not cheerleading is a sport."

Going to Toronto was going to be awesome. Besides the cheer championship—which we were doing as a warm-up to Ontario provincials—we had plans to go shopping and out for dinner in Chinatown. Arielle was excited about visiting the North York Art Gallery. It was going to be a great time.

"I'll miss you when I'm in Toronto, Liam," I told him as we rode home from Eliza's.

Liam shrugged. "You'll have more fun without me anyway."

"That's not true," I said, even though it was.

He laughed.

"What?" I asked.

"That wasn't very convincing."

I took a deep breath. Was he asking for a fight? We'd needed to talk for ages, but there was always a reason we couldn't. He wasn't in the mood, or I was at practice, or we couldn't get any time alone. But now we were in the privacy of his car with twenty minutes of driving before we'd reach Stratford. I looked down at the buckle on my purse. "Well...," I began, "you know I love you, Liam. But I don't know what's up with you lately."

"Not you too, Marnie."

"Me too what?" I tried to ignore the irritation in his voice.

"You know my mom's been hassling me lately. Saying I'm depressed and all that garbage. I don't need you jumping on the bandwagon."

"But you did admit you're a bit depressed," I reminded him. "You know, before Christmas. We talked about it."

He stared at the road ahead. "It's winter. It gets dark at five thirty. Who isn't depressed this time of year?"

"You weren't depressed this time last year."

He stayed silent.

"You can talk to me," I told him gently. "I've known you for so long..."

"And if there were an actual problem," he said, "I would."

"Well," I said, "maybe the fact that your attitude is stressing me out counts as an 'actual problem.'"

He pulled the car over so hard that it fishtailed and then spun out, leaving us facing in the direction we had come from. It happened so fast that I didn't have a chance to scream. We'd been stopped for more than thirty seconds before I realized I'd been holding my breath.

"Get out," Liam said.

"Wh—what?" I stammered. "But it's dark—"

"You won't be waiting around long," he said. "One of your stupid cheerleading friends will be right along to rescue you as usual."

My hands shaking, I reached for my purse and lifted it onto my lap. I put my hand on the door latch. "What's the name of this road?" I asked, as calmly as I could.

"What?"

"The name of this road," I repeated. "So I can explain where I am."

He looked at me with an expression on his face I'd never seen before. "This would be the end of the road," he said. "And by the way, Marnie, the reason I wasn't depressed the same time last year is that my life wasn't halfway down the frigging toilet then."

"You mean the scholarship?" I asked, but he didn't hear me. He slammed the car door, spun the car around and sped off.

chapter eight

I called my dad, not Arielle, to pick me up. Liam had been so much of a jerk, leaving me out there in the cold, that I was almost embarrassed for him. I wasn't ready to deal with Arielle's outrage on my behalf.

My dad was so worried about me that he got there in less than ten minutes. I climbed, shivering, into his car.

"Are you okay?" he asked. "Did he hurt you?"

I shook my head.

"What happened?"

I shrugged. "I don't even know. I don't even know what I did!"

"Forget him," Dad said in a tone so firm that I knew the conversation was over. But when we drove past a farmhouse outside Brocksden, there was a car that looked like Liam's parked near the end of the driveway. After we passed it, the car pulled out and followed us, staying a long way behind. Liam had been watching to make sure someone came for me.

When we got back to our house, it was almost midnight. Too late to call Arielle. I dropped my coat over the back of the sofa and stumbled upstairs to my bedroom.

I needed to get into my room, sit down and pull myself together.

I climbed, fully dressed, onto the middle of my bed. I sat there in the dark for a long time, trying to decide whether or not to sneak back downstairs to the computer. I thought maybe Ari might be up and online. She'd been on the computer an awful lot lately.

I knew that Liam would not have wanted me to tell Arielle about his problems, but how could he expect me to cope with this all alone? I loved him, and I was afraid for him. He had always been the levelheaded one in our relationship. He was supposed to be the one looking out for me. Tears welled up in my eyes, and I pressed my forehead against my knees.

When I opened my eyes again, it was morning. I was shivering. I'd slept in my clothes on top of the comforter. I climbed stiffly to my feet and started getting ready for school. With the Great Lakes Championship fast approaching, we had cheerleading practice again that night. Coach Saylor had explained that we had a lot of fine-tuning to do if we hoped to do well. She hadn't looked at me when she said it, which was kind. Using the expression "fine-tuning" to describe me figuring out how to ace a stunt more than fifty percent of the time was kind too. She'd already cut me all the slack that she could.

After dinner I scrambled to catch the early crosstown bus. I wanted to get to the cheer club as soon as I could, so Arielle and I would have time to talk before too many other girls got there. Ari could always be counted on to arrive early.

Except this time, she didn't. Everybody else trickled in and got changed. Eventually I had to move out into the studio with the rest of them. Coach Saylor announced that Arielle was sick and that she wasn't coming. I almost started to cry right there.

After warm-up, we split up into our stunt groups. I was so absorbed in my breakup with Liam and my disappointment over Arielle being away that I didn't notice at first that something was wrong. The first time I bobbled a lift, Amy Jo wouldn't look me in the eye. When I looked first at Priya, and then at Lucy, each girl gave me a weak little smile. The kind of smile you give a person who's about to be fired or kicked off an island or maybe cut from a team.

"What's up?" I asked, trying to keep my voice casual.

"What do you mean?" Amy Jo answered in a voice that made it clear she was hiding something.

With Arielle away, Lucy was the closest thing I had to an ally. She was new, and I'd been nice to her. She'd gone with Arielle and me to Ashleigh's party. So I asked for her help putting the mats away, and I cornered her in the storeroom. "Lucy, I know something's going on. Amy Jo can't lie to save her life. What's up?"

"It's Shona," she said. "She's going around talking to everyone about you."

"What's she saying?"

She gave me a sympathetic look. "She's trying to convince them to talk to Coach Saylor. As a group. About replacing you."

I felt a lightness at the pit of my stomach, like I was on an elevator dropping too fast.

"Don't worry," Lucy said. "A lot of the girls stood up for you. Most of them. All of the ones in our group. Including Amy Jo."

I considered asking her which girls hadn't stood up for me. But what difference did it make? They were right. I was awful.

Lucy hugged me, quickly, as if she was afraid someone might see us. "It's okay, Marnie. You're going to get up to speed. We could practice on the weekend again, if you want."

I nodded. "I'd like that."

"So what are you going to do about Shona?" she asked as we walked away from the club.

I shrugged. "I don't know. I guess maybe I should talk to her." I would deal with things directly. I wouldn't go behind her back, the way Shona did to me.

I didn't have to wait long for my opportunity. Without Arielle to drive me, I had to take the bus home. Shona was waiting too.

Unlike Amy Jo, Shona had no problem looking me in the eye. When I walked down the steps, she moved toward me. She stood right next to me under the roof over-hang, like we were old friends.

"Hi," I said casually.

"Hi, Marnie," she answered.

We stood in silence for a couple of minutes.

This is stupid, I thought. She's just a kid. Talk to her.

I took a deep breath. "So, Shona," I asked, "why wouldn't you come to me, if you have a problem with me?"

She turned toward me, her face framed by the pink fur trim of her parka. I could tell she was thinking about what to say. To her credit, she hadn't done what I'd expected her to do, which was deny she had trash-talked me behind my back.

"Well?" I asked.

"Well," she said, "I didn't think there was anything you could do about it."

"About what?"

She shrugged. "Your stunts. Either you can get them right, or you can't."

"And you think I can't."

She didn't answer. She just smiled a little fake-sympathetic smile.

"I only took Emma's place two weeks ago," I said. "I need time to get up to speed. I can't believe you're already trying to get Coach to replace me."

She gave me a funny look, but said nothing.

"What?" I asked, running out of patience.

"Well," she said, "were you ever any good? Like, the last time you were a flyer?" She looked at me, her blue eyes wide. "Which was, what, two years ago?"

I frowned. "As a matter of fact," I said, "I was. Very good."

"Then why didn't Coach keep you as a flyer when you made level five?"

I could feel the blood pounding in my ears. I wanted to punch her in the face. I'd never felt so angry with anyone in my whole life.

I heard the rumble of the bus as it made its way up the street, and I knew I didn't want to be on the same bus as Shona Bart. I took two steps backward.

"Even if you were good once," she said, moving toward the bus, "it doesn't mean you're any good now. You're holding us all back, Marnie," she said. She stepped onto the bus, and the doors closed behind her, leaving me in the cold and the deepening dark.

chapter nine

I called my mom to tell her I'd be late. Then I got on the east-end bus instead of my own. I had to speak with Arielle. My whole life was falling to pieces, and she was my best friend. Even though she was sick, I knew I could count on her to make me feel better. I certainly couldn't feel any worse. To keep from crying in front of the people on the bus, I stared out the window at the gray February streets.

When I got to Arielle's house, her mom ushered me in. I always knock on the front door instead of Arielle's side door after dark. I don't want to startle her parents by setting off the security lights.

"How's Arielle feeling?" I asked.

Mrs. Kuypers looked momentarily confused. "Feeling? Oh yes. She did say something about a headache. But go on in."

I took off my wet boots and walked down the hall to Arielle's suite.

"Hmm?" she answered when I knocked on the door.

I let myself in. "Hi," I said.

Arielle was hunched over her laptop, typing.

"Oh, hey, Marnie," she said without turning around.

"One sec, okay?"

She typed a couple more lines, then swiveled around in her chair so that her body was blocking the screen. I sat across from her on the bed.

"How are you feeling?" I asked.

"Fine," she said. "I had the most horrible headache earlier."

"You blew off practice because of a headache?"

She frowned. "I wasn't feeling well, Marnie. What's the big deal?"

"Oh, only that Shona is trying to get me kicked off the team."

"What?" she asked. "What did you do?"

"I didn't do anything," I said. "She's right. I stink."

"No, you don't."

"I do. I can't even do a split throw without falling on my face."

Arielle sighed. "Marnie," she said, "no matter what Shona says, Coach Saylor is not going to replace you. Think about it. Who would she replace you with?"

"Oh," I said, "so it's not that I'm good, it's just that there's no one else?"

Arielle didn't take the bait. She just stared at me until a ping from her laptop caught her attention. She turned around quickly and shut the lid.

"Who was that?" I asked.

She hesitated. "Can you keep a secret?"

"Of course!" I said.

"Have you ever heard of Trey Benedict?"

I shook my head.

"He's an artist," Arielle said. "A really good one. He's had shows in some of the best galleries in New York. And he's looking at my work." Her eyes sparkled with excitement.

I did my best to smile. "What do you mean, 'looking at'? Like, critiquing?"

Arielle nodded. "I sent him that portfolio you reviewed for me."

"And? What did he say?" I could tell the answer by the look on her face.

"He liked it," she said.

I smiled, for real this time. "Of course he did, Ari. Your paintings are amazing."

She got out of her chair and hugged me. "Thanks. I'm so excited, Marnie!"

It was nice to be hugged. I needed it. I made room for her beside me on the bed. "So," I asked, "what does this mean, exactly?"

"Um...," she began, and then she shrugged. "Well...nothing right now, I guess." She was silent for a moment. "It's good to be recognized by someone who's objective, don't you think? Someone who doesn't know me."

"Absolutely," I said. "I'm sorry if I don't sound very excited. It's been a rough few days."

She nodded. "And I'm sorry I wasn't at practice today. I had no idea Shona would go this far. I'll call Coach about it, okay?"

"No!" I exclaimed. "Don't. I'll deal with it myself."

Arielle nodded her approval. "That's the best way. And don't let it get to you so much, okay? It's not like you to be so rattled."

I shook my head. "It's not just the cheerleading thing though. There's something else."

She listened while I told her about Liam dumping me at the side of the road.

"At night, in the middle of winter?"

I nodded.

"What a jerk!" she said. "Stay away from him, Marnie."

"But we've been together two years," I said. "How could he turn his back on all that?"

"Marnie! Are you crazy? He left you by the side of the road."

I was starting to regret having told her anything. I knew what Liam had done was terrible, but it was out of character for him. Liam was a good person. Even Arielle used to like him, and she was very picky about guys. Did she really think I could shrug off two years of dating like it was a failed experiment? Sometimes Arielle could be incredibly cold. "He's depressed, Ari. He's just not himself."

She frowned. "We're in high school, Marnie. Liam's in his last year, like me. There's university coming up. And then this brutal job market. Plus parents who still think they can tell us exactly what to do with our lives. Who isn't a little bit crazy right now? But it doesn't give him an excuse to treat you like garbage just because you have your act together."

She was right. She was so right. Like always.

"So you don't think he needs help?" I asked. "You don't think I should tell someone?"

"Liam's problems are none of your concern anymore."

"It just seems so cold," I said, "to just write someone off like that and walk away. I guess he wanted that scholarship really badly. He was probably afraid to talk about it in case it didn't happen. And now, who is he going to talk to about it? We were best friends. I can't stop caring about him just like that!"

She gave me a look I didn't like. The way my mother looks at me when she thinks she has all the answers. "Forget about it. You have your own life to worry about, Marnie."

chapter ten

True to her word, Arielle didn't say anything to Coach Saylor about Shona and me.
But at our Saturday practice, she made me
assistant captain.

"Any objections?" she asked, looking
around at the other girls.

After a long moment, Ashleigh pointed
out that we'd never had an assistant captain
before.

Arielle shrugged. "The Great Lakes
entry form has a space for the name of an

assistant captain. I guess it's in case I can't be reached or something. Makes sense."

It was my turn to look around at the group. Which girls had Shona turned against me? Which ones were on my side? I couldn't tell.

Casually, as if it were an afterthought, Arielle added, "We don't need to vote on this or anything, do we? Marnie's a veteran on this team. We all know how much she's done for us. She never misses a practice, she helps all of us with our tumbling, she choreographed most of the 'Midsummer' routine—"

"Go, Marnie," said Priya. Lucy and a couple of the others nodded in support.

"Hear, hear," said Jada.

"Congratulations, Marnie!" said Keri, the group-three flyer.

One by one, the girls made their way over to hug me or give me a high five. Arielle caught my eye, and I smiled, grateful for her support. I had a lot to learn if I was ever going to be the kind of leader she was, but I'd always have her example to follow.

My promotion boosted my confidence. After the warm-up, we practiced the opening section of our "Midsummer" routine, the one we had planned for the first day of competition at Great Lakes. There's a turning arabesque just ten seconds in. It was a stunt that I remembered Emma being nervous about, because it came up before you had a chance to shake off the run-on jitters. Not only did I have to do an arabesque—a one-leg, no-hands lift—but I had to hold it steady while the spotters pivoted a quick half-turn.

I waited at my corner, heart pounding, while Coach Saylor hit Play on the CD player. "Sweetness" by Jimmy Eat World started up. "If you're listening..." Since our group had the farthest to run, Priya and Lucy charged across the mats, with Amy Jo and me close behind them. I lined up squarely, and, right on cue, the bases straightened their arms. Amy Jo bounced me up onto the platform Priya and Lucy had made with their hands. Stomach muscles tight, I extended my left leg and squared my shoulders. I locked my gaze on my own image in the mirror. Be strong, Marnie, I prayed. No wobbling. The bases pivoted, and I held my own. When they stopped, I was staring straight at the space between Shona's shoulder blades. And I was as steady as she was.

"Sing it back…" The girls lowered me to the ground.

I felt so pumped after that. I aced nearly every other stunt we did. I put the image of Emma's fall right out of my mind. I forgot about the ground below me. I forgot about Shona and her stupid plot to get rid of me. I balanced on the bases' palms and shoulders as if posing in thin air was the most natural thing to do.

It felt great.

I walked out of the club on such a high that I walked right by Liam's car without noticing it. He had to start the engine and follow me down the sidewalk.

"Hey!" he called, leaning out the window.

I turned around, surprised, and then, remembering Arielle's advice, I turned away and kept on walking.

"Hop in," he called out.

"No, thanks," I said.

Arielle hurried up until she was even with me, and the two of us walked resolutely toward her car. Liam sat in the idling car for a moment, then drove slowly away.

chapter eleven

Two weeks later, I was sitting next to Arielle on the bus to Toronto.

We'd left Stratford just after nine. Registration for the competition didn't start until four, but since it was February, Coach Saylor hadn't wanted to take any chances with the driving conditions.

I looked out the window. Black fields stretched out for miles, splotched in places with melting patches of snow. The reeds that stuck out here and there looked like they'd been dead forever. There were no signs of spring.

The scene on the bus, by contrast, was like Spring Break in Florida. The girls bounced, chattering, from seat to seat. Knapsacks were opened, and snacks were passed around. Hip-hop music blared from somebody's stereo. The situation was approaching mayhem, but Coach Saylor was up at the front, hooked into her iPod. Arielle made no attempt to calm the girls down either; in fact, she had a huge smile on her face.

I was glad to see her so happy. She had seemed distant lately. She wasn't nearly as psyched about competition season this year as she had been in the past. I'd wondered if it was because of the pressure to win provincials. In the past, when she was under pressure, Arielle got more involved, not less. This year she seemed to be pulling back from cheerleading a little bit. It was reassuring to see her as excited as the others on this trip.

A camera flash blinded me. When I could

see again, Keri was leaning over the seat, checking out my picture in her cell phone.

"Wow, Marnie, not so flattering!" she laughed. I looked and saw that my eyes were closed, and my mouth was hanging open.

"Erase it!" I said.

"Sure thing," she said, frantically punching keys while trying to keep the phone out of reach of my grabbing hands. "But it's already on Facebook."

"You're kidding, right?" I asked.

Arielle shook her head. "She's bluffing."

"I am not!" Keri said.

"Keri," said Lucy, "don't forget. You and I are sharing a room. Just hope you don't drool or anything in your sleep..." Lucy mimed snapping a picture.

Keri laughed and turned around in her seat. I reached across Arielle toward Lucy's bag of chips.

"Uh-uh!" Lucy said. "No chips for you. I have to lift you over my head, remember?"

I grabbed some chips anyway. I don't gain weight no matter what I eat. Too much nervous energy.

But today it was the good, excited kind of nervousness. My performance had improved steadily over the previous two weeks, and I was feeling better about myself. I'd taken Arielle's advice, and I'd practiced the entire routines—not just the stunt parts—all the way through, over and over. Arielle told me that knowing the routine so well you could do it in your sleep was the best thing you could do for your nerves. Then, even if you were really freaking out, your body could perform on autopilot.

The Great Lakes Championship required two routines. First there was a three-minute qualifier, which we would perform on Friday afternoon. Then there was a longer free-style event on Saturday. The short routine was "Midsummer." The long routine was "Groovy." I knew both routines solid. Whether I could execute them perfectly was another matter. But I could stick all the stunts in practice at least 90 percent of the time, which was the best you could ask for. Level-five stunts are tough. Once in a while they fall apart. But if you don't attempt the tough stunts, you can't get the top scores. You need to take the risks if you want the glory.

We made great time and arrived in Toronto two hours too early to check in to our hotel. Coach Saylor rounded us up in the lobby for a head count.

"All here," she said. "Good. We have until three. What do you girls want to do?"

We ended up going shopping at the Eaton Centre. We split up into groups of three or four, with instructions to meet up at three o'clock at a coffee place we'd spotted. Arielle, Lucy, Ashleigh and I were the first ones at the meeting spot. We bought fancy hot chocolates and then stood looking around for a big enough table.

There was one near the front, but a trio of guys had backed their chairs into one side of it so that they could look out the window. Arielle moved toward them.

"May I?" she asked.

The closest guy was the hottest. He had dark blond hair, straight white teeth and a tan that suggested he'd recently been away somewhere warm. He smiled and moved his chair, making a sweeping gesture toward the table, like he was the host of the place.

Arielle smiled, but sat down with her back to him. The rest of us joined her, talking in hushed tones.

"Uh, good seats," said Ashleigh. "Nice view."

Lucy and I giggled.

A few minutes into our conversation, another of the cute guys, this one with slicked-back wavy hair, leaned toward us. "You girls on a field trip?"

"What makes you think that?" asked Ashleigh.

"Too young to be out of high school... too classy to be dropouts."

Lucy and I giggled again.

"We're on a road trip," explained Ashleigh. "Cheerleading competition. What about you?"

"Basketball tournament," said Nice Teeth. "We're from Ottawa. Carleton University. You?"

We explained that we were from Stratford, which, of course, they'd barely heard of. But we discovered, to everyone's surprise, we were all staying at the same hotel.

"Well," said Wavy Hair, "I'll take that as a sign."

"A sign of what?" squeaked Lucy.

"A sign that you girls were destined to come to our game tonight. To cheer us on. And then join us afterward for the victory celebration."

"Who says you'll win?" shot back Arielle, without turning around in her chair to face him.

"Oh, we'll win," said Nice Teeth.

Back at the hotel, Arielle and I got dressed for dinner. "So," I said, "are we going to that basketball game later? Ashleigh looked it up on Google Maps. It's close. Probably three bucks each by cab."

Arielle smoothed an already-perfect eyebrow. "We won't get back from dinner until eight."

I shrugged. "We'd be, like, twenty minutes late for the game. It would be fine."

She didn't look convinced. "There's some stuff I need to do tonight on my laptop. Email and stuff. But you can go without me, Mar. I know Lucy and Ashleigh want to go."

I was disappointed. How many chances would I get to hang out with hot university guys? Arielle was going to university next year. Maybe that was why it was no big deal to her. But I had a whole year to wait. And these weren't only university guys, they were basketball players. It was bad enough that I didn't have Liam to hang around with anymore. But Arielle? She and I used to have so much fun...

I ended up going with Lucy, Ashleigh and six other girls from our team. By the time I got back to the room at midnight—Coach's curfew—Arielle was already asleep.

When I woke up in the morning, she was gone.

chapter twelve

There were a dozen reasonable explanations for Arielle's empty bed, but it didn't matter. I panicked. The moment I realized she was gone, a bad feeling washed over me. I banged on the door next to ours, and Ashleigh answered. "She probably just went for a jog," she mumbled.

"In downtown Toronto? I don't think so."

Sharon appeared behind Ashleigh in the doorway, wearing pajamas in a monkey-

and-banana pattern. "What's wrong?" she asked.

"Arielle's not in the room, and Marnie's all freaked out," said Ashleigh.

"Wasn't she with you two last night?" Sharon asked. "Maybe she snuck out in the middle of the night with one of those ball players!"

Ashleigh rolled her eyes at me. Sharon loved a scandal. Even if she had to make one up.

I shook my head. "Arielle wasn't even with us at the basketball game last night. Don't make this worse, Sharon, just for your own entertainment."

Sharon made a face at me like I'd hurt her feelings. As if her feelings even mattered at a time like this.

I had to alert Coach Saylor. I ducked back into my room and dressed as fast as I could. By the time I came out, a small crowd of cheerleaders in pajamas stood in the hall outside my door.

"What's going on?" asked Jada.

"Ari's gone." I fought my way through the pack, striding quickly toward room 208, which Coach was sharing with one of the chaperones.

"What do you mean, gone?" Jada said.

"Gone, as in not here," I snapped.

"Did she take all her stuff?"

Amy Jo's question stopped me in my tracks. I thought back to the room I'd just left. There'd been a blue skirt hanging in the closet and a bottle of contact lens solution on the counter.

"No," I answered, suddenly relieved. "Her stuff's still there."

When I talked to Coach Saylor, she pointed out that it was eight in the morning. Arielle wasn't even late for breakfast yet. "She should have said where she was going," Coach acknowledged, "but I've known Arielle a long time. Sometimes she needs space. Head back to your rooms and get dressed. Meet me in the restaurant at eight thirty. I'm sure Arielle will be back soon."

The girls straggled away, leaving me feeling a bit sheepish. But I couldn't shake the bad feeling, no matter what anyone said.

Arielle did not come back for breakfast. And, she was not back in time for our ten-thirty bus to the conference center.

And, even worse, Arielle hadn't left behind all of her stuff. She'd left a suitcase, the skirt and the lens cleaner, but her makeup bag was gone and so were her laptop, her purse, her boots and her coat. All the important stuff.

It almost seemed as though Arielle had left the suitcase as a decoy. To avoid suspicion long enough to get away.

Once we figured that out, the real panic set in.

We left the bus idling outside for half an hour while we searched the hotel, knocking on doors, asking questions, handing out Coach's cell phone number to anyone who would take it. Since Arielle had left with her boots and her coat, we knew we were unlikely to find her inside, but we had to try. Finally, when we couldn't wait any longer and still make our competition slot on time, the chaperones herded all the girls onto the bus.

Some of the girls were whispering nervously. Others were silent. A few, like Sharon and Amy Jo, were crying. Realizing that we needed something distracting to do, Ms. Wilkinson—Keri's mom—suggested we do each other's hair. For competitions, we wear ponytails with ribbons in red, white and black, our team colors. Every Soar team wears black and white with one accent color. I fumbled hopelessly with Priya's fine, shiny hair. It kept slipping out of my fingers before I could get the elastic on.

"This is ridiculous!" I said, letting go of her hair and the ribbons. "Arielle is missing. Out there!" I pointed out the bus window at the unfamiliar city, with its graffiti-covered walls and crawling traffic. "And we're doing each other's hair and heading for a stupid competition like nothing has happened? We should—"

"Now, Marnie," interrupted Ms. Wilkinson, "your coach is at the hotel right now, on the phone with the police—"

"But we should be helping!" said Lucy. "We should be looking for her!"

Ms. Wilkinson shook her head and spoke sternly. "No. Nobody leaves. This is a serious situation. We will not have another girl separated from this group. Do I make myself clear?"

Sharon let out a loud, choking sob.

Ms. Wilkinson softened. "I know it seems strange to be going into a competition at a time like this. I know it doesn't seem important compared to finding Arielle. But there's nothing more you girls can safely do to help." She bent down and scooped up Priya's tangled ribbons. "You searched the hotel. Now you need to stay together."

Ashleigh nodded her agreement. I marveled at her calmness. I'd never realized that bad situations bring out the best in natural leaders. I wished I was more like Ashleigh.

"You came here to perform," Ms. Wilkinson continued. "It's better than sitting around the hotel in hysterics. So that's what we're going to do."

Ms. Wilkinson reached for Priya's hairbrush, and I handed it over. Then I leaned forward, my head in my hands, while she finished my job.

chapter thirteen

Running away on the eve of a competition was the very last thing you would expect from Arielle. I looked out the bus window. Traffic was gridlocked on the roads, and people pushed past each other on the sidewalk. Busy city people, disappearing up side streets and into buildings with bars on the windows. Even the kids I saw looked tough. One boy a few years younger than me coasted dangerously close to the bus on a bike. He wore no helmet and steered expertly around the February slush piles, putting one hand on the side of the bus for stability. We were three hours' drive from Stratford, but Toronto could have been on another planet. It was so different from our little town. And Arielle was alone out there.

Maybe she'd run out to do an errand and had gotten lost.

With her computer and her makeup bag? No.

The bus squealed to a stop, interrupting my thoughts. I fell into step behind the other girls, lining up numbly in front of the baggage door to wait for my gym bag. I turned around when I felt a hand on my shoulder.

"Marnie," said Ms. Wilkinson softly.

I looked up.

She beckoned for me to take a couple of steps away from the others, and then she spoke. "I know you're worried about your friend. But you're our assistant captain. These girls are going to need some leadership if they're going to get through this competition. Are you up to it?"

I nodded, but I wasn't convinced.

We walked in almost complete silence into the conference center. The lobby was packed with cheerleaders, most wearing their team ribbons and stage makeup. The girls—and a few boys—were talking and laughing, bubbling over with anticipation. It was the kind of exciting, charged environment you experience only at competitions. It was an environment that I usually loved. This was a moment that I'd always dreamed about: my first time arriving to compete as a flyer.

But that morning, my team walked into the conference center with all the energy of a shell-shocked band of disaster survivors. Arielle had been the head and heart of our team. Losing her felt like a knockout punch. We were acting like a broken team.

Ashleigh, who was a step ahead of the group, turned around and stared at me. I shrugged my shoulders at her. What?

She looked away in frustration and then shouted, "Starlings! This way! Team meeting!"

We pushed our way through the crowd, following Ashleigh's long auburn ponytail. We walked until we found our team's gathering spot, marked off with tape on the lobby floor. Some people were sitting in our spot, and it was so loud and crowded that it would have been impossible to talk there. Ashleigh led us through a curtain and into the auditorium seating area. We followed her up three flights of steps to the empty top tier of seats. Even with the competition going on below us, it was quieter there than in the lobby.

"Sit," Ashleigh said.

All twelve of us sat.

"Not you, Marnie," she whispered.

Oh, right. I was the assistant captain. I stood up, and Ashleigh took my seat.

"Uh...," I began, "...like Ms. Wilkinson said on the bus...I know it feels weird, being here without Ari. But she...um...would have wanted us to compete..."

Shona, who'd been unusually quiet all day, piped up. "Then why isn't she here?"

"Pardon?" I asked. The other girls turned and stared at Shona.

But Shona was not deterred. "How could she ditch us a few hours before we're supposed to go on?"

"Well, obviously," I answered, "nobody—"

"Everybody talks about Arielle like she can do no wrong," said Shona. "But look at us. We go on in forty minutes. We're short a base. Sharon won't stop blubbering. Nobody's warmed up. What kind of captain does this to her team?"

I stared at her, my mouth hanging open.

"I can't believe you think this competition is more important than Arielle's safety!" Lucy said.

"Oh, come on," Shona said. "Arielle's safe. She's probably on the number fifty-two bus right now, going to some art gallery. She blew us off."

"She did not!" I said.

"She did," said Shona. "And don't pretend you weren't in on it. Why else would she make you assistant captain?"

"Shona," I said, fighting to keep my anger under control, "if I had any idea where Arielle was, do you really think I would keep it secret?"

Ashleigh jumped to her feet. "Enough! All of you. If we have any hope of getting this done, we have to focus on cheerleading. Sharon, can you take Arielle's place in stunt group three?"

Sharon was a tumbler. The way the routine was choreographed, she wasn't tied to any stunt group, though she sometimes acted as spotter.

"How should I know?" Sharon wailed. "I don't know Ari's part!"

Besides, I thought, she was hysterical. If I were Keri, the group-three flyer, I wouldn't want to put my safety in Sharon's shaky hands.

"I'll do it," volunteered Jada. Like Ashleigh, Jada was one of the few girls who were handling this whole situation with some maturity and composure. The way I was supposed to be handling it, as assistant captain.

Arielle wasn't even there, and I'd still managed to let her down.

Ashleigh nodded. "Thank you, Jada. Now we'll find an empty spot in the hall to stretch, and then I'll ask the organizers if they'll let us into the on-deck room a few minutes early. Maybe they'll be understanding."

The on-deck room at this competition was not really a room. It was the southernmost third of the stadium floor. It was divided from the north side by a high curtain, put up to hide the sound equipment and to provide a backdrop to the performance mats. There were mats on the south side too, but these were reserved for teams warming up. Normally, they don't let you into the warm-up area until about fifteen minutes before you go on. Some creative begging on Ashleigh's part got us a little corner where we could work out the choreography changes made necessary by Arielle's disappearance.

Lucy, Priya and I lined up in front of Keri's stunt group so that Jada could copy Lucy's positioning. Being a good base meant knowing two things—where to place your hands for the lifts and throws, and how to time all your movements with the flyer's momentum. Jada had been a base before Emma's accident. Every competition song has its own rhythm, and each stunt group has its own particular signals, apart from the usual beat-counting, to communicate timing.

With Jada and the rest of group three watching, I performed the slow turning arabesque from "Midsummer," and then the tuck throw from "Groovy" while the rest of the girls counted the beats. It wasn't until Lucy and Priya put me down that I realized I hadn't felt nervous doing the stunts. In fact, I hadn't thought about my own performance at all. I'd just concentrated on keeping my movements precise so that Jada could follow Lucy.

Maybe that was the trick—to stop thinking so much about myself as a performer and more about how I fit in with the team. Maybe that was how girls like Ashleigh and Jada—and Arielle, of course—stayed so calm.

chapter fourteen

Despite my own little discovery, the ten minutes of extra practice in the on-deck room didn't make any difference. We could have practiced all day, and we still would have stunk. We moved like a band of zombies out there.

When we walked off the mats, Coach Saylor was waiting for us. Some of the girls barely even looked up at her.

"Cheer up," Coach said. "At least you got it done, right? That shows a lot of spunk."

"Any news about Arielle?" Jada asked, ignoring the coach's praise.

Coach shook her head. "Not yet. We had her parents email a photo to the police..."

"But?" I asked, knowing she was holding something back.

"Well, girls, Arielle is eighteen. The Toronto police, and our police back home too, consider her to be an adult. Unless there's evidence of foul play—and there isn't—they won't start searching until forty-eight hours have passed."

"What?" Ashleigh exclaimed. "She's alone in a city she doesn't know."

Coach nodded. "Her parents are frantic. They're on their way down. But Arielle's turned off her phone. And other details have come to light"—she hesitated for a moment—"that suggest she might not want to be found."

No one spoke. A cold, heavy feeling settled into the pit of my stomach. "What other details?" I asked, quietly.

"Well, contrary to what she told her parents, Arielle never submitted her application for university residence. And she's not the type to miss deadlines. Her parents are worried that she's given up on going to U of T next fall."

I thought back to the end of January and Arielle's vague answers to my questions about residence. Why hadn't I pressed her? I'd been so wrapped up in my struggles as a flyer, and my problems with Liam, that I'd missed the signs that something big was going on with Arielle.

I slumped to my knees on the sidelines. Would I have been able to stop her if I'd taken the time to ask some questions?

"You okay, Marnie?" Coach Saylor asked.

I nodded without looking up.

"You know," said Ms. Wilkinson, "you girls didn't eat much at breakfast. What do they sell at the snack bar?"

Coach reached into her pocket for money. "Priya, Samara, Amy Jo, why don't you head up to the snack bar and see if you can get some pizzas? And some sports drinks."

The girls took the money and headed off. The rest of us sat down on the sidelines.

A few girls were whispering about Coach's news, but the majority stayed quiet, watching the remainder of the morning's competition groups without real interest. The Friday morning results were to be announced at 1:00 PM. After that, we'd be free to go back to our hotel. With the performance we'd given, we'd probably missed the cut anyway. We wouldn't be needed for Saturday's round. We could go straight back to Stratford today, if we wanted to.

With that thought to comfort me, I sat obediently and waited for my pizza. I tried not to think about Arielle on some crowded street—or bus—all alone.

Bus...What had Shona meant when she mentioned the number fifty-two bus? Was it a real bus, or was she making it up? I promised myself I'd ask her about it when I got the chance.

To our surprise, when the judges announced the morning results, we found out we'd tied for third in our division. It was far below what we were capable of, but still good enough to qualify for the Saturday round. When they called our team name, we were so sure we'd been eliminated that only Shona and a couple of other girls jumped up to run out onto the mats to get their ribbons. Shona stood there next to one of the judges and glared at the rest of us until we finally clambered to our feet and walked on.

Yay, I thought. Third place.

When I got back to the sidelines, I saw Sharon and Barb whispering to Coach Saylor. Coach put a hand on Sharon's shoulder and turned her around to face us.

"Girls," Coach said, "I understand that, in light of Arielle's disappearance, some of you are eager to get home. Barb and Sharon have asked that we withdraw from tomorrow's competition. Quitting is not usually an option for a Soar team. But as we discussed last month, we enrolled in this competition as a warm-up for provincials. Based on our standing today, the best finish we could attain, if we stayed for tomorrow's round, would be third place.

And we'd need to be close to perfect to do that. So I'm going to put it to a vote. Girls in favor of withdrawing, please raise your hands."

Ten hands went up, and I could see that Amy Jo, one of the three holdouts with Shona and me, was wavering. Lucy elbowed her in the ribs. "The sooner we get home," Lucy whispered, "the sooner we can start calling around to Arielle's friends."

Amy Jo looked away from Shona and raised her hand. Shona and I were the only holdouts.

"That's eleven out of thirteen," said Coach. "I'll go talk to the judges."

Before we left town, we used Jada's laptop and the photo Ari's parents had sent to put together a Missing Person poster. We had a bunch printed at a copy shop, and we plastered them all over the conference center and the neighborhood near the hotel. While we were postering, I sidled up to Shona.

"What was that bus you were talking about?"

"What bus?" She frowned at me, obviously still furious that we'd pulled out of the competition.

"You said Arielle was probably on the number fifty-two bus already. Is that a real bus? How do you know about it?"

"It's the northbound bus. To the art gallery. You know, for the field trip that Arielle cared about more than she cared about this competition."

I ignored the dig. "But how do you know about that bus?"

"My grandparents live in Stouffville," she said. "Not far from here. They used to take me to a store in North York to buy my gymnastics outfits. For competitions."

Well, I thought, aren't you special. But all I said was, "Oh."

chapter fifteen

It was 7:00 PM by the time we reached Stratford. After our night out with the basketball players, and the long day's drama, it felt like midnight to me. It was a relief to see my father's car pull into the Soar Club lot. Dad got out to load my bags. To my surprise, he gave me a long, tight hug before climbing back into the car. I guess the news of Arielle's disappearance hit close to home.

"Are you hungry, hon?" he asked. "Want to hit a drive-thru or something?"

"No, thanks," I said. "I just want to go home to bed."

"I should warn you, sweetie," my dad said, "we got a call from the police. They want you to come to the station tomorrow for an interview."

"Do I have to?" I asked.

"Well," he said, "I'm not sure you have to. But I guess they think you could be of some help, if they decide to start a search."

"Okay," I sighed.

A couple of hours later, I was watching TV in my pajamas when the phone rang. It was Arielle's mother, calling for me. She wanted to know if I could come by to talk. "Her paintings are gone, Marnie," she told me.

I went up to my room to change back into my clothes.

"Where are you going, sweetie?" asked my mom.

"Ari's mother wants to talk to me," I said. "Can you drive me over there?"

I'd tried to keep the fatigue out of my voice, but I couldn't hide those things from my mom. She put her arms around me in the hallway, and then she held me out at arm's length. "Listen, Marnie, you tell Mrs. Kuypers that if there's anything I can do to help, she should give me a call. I can't imagine what she's going through right now."

I nodded in agreement and then stepped out the door to warm up the car for my mom. When I got to the Kuypers' house, Arielle's mom looked as elegant and well groomed as ever, but her hands were shaking. She led me into the living room, where Mr. Kuypers was waiting, and we sat stiffly across from each other. The last time I had been in that room, Arielle and I had been sprawled on the floor, our feet up on the couch cushions. We'd just come in from a long run. It was September, the beginning of cheerleading season, and we'd been trying to whip ourselves into shape. We were laughing at how winded we were and talking happily about the season to come.

What a difference a few months can make, I thought as I sat across from Ari's worried parents.

"So she told you she'd applied for residence?" Mrs. Kuypers asked. "Actually applied?"

I tried to remember Arielle's exact words. "I'm not sure," I said. "I think she just told me she'd make up her mind later."

"And you say you didn't help her pack for this Toronto trip? You don't remember how many bags she had?"

I shook my head. Clearly, my focus had been on one person only: me. "When did you notice the paintings were gone?" I asked.

"This afternoon," Mr. Kuypers said "As soon as I got the call from your coach, I drove home from work and checked Arielle's room. The outside doors were all locked, as usual. But the paintings were gone. There was a roll of packing tape on the floor. Whoever took the paintings had to have had a van and a key."

And they wouldn't have been spotted, I realized. The Kuypers' driveway went all the way around to the back of the house. Whoever took the paintings would have gone in and out the side door to Arielle's studio. It wasn't visible from the road.

"And she didn't say anything to you about any unusual plans?" asked Mrs. Kuypers. "Nothing at all?"

Both of them stared at me, disappointment written all over their faces. "You're her best friend...," Mr. Kuypers said.

"She didn't tell me anything," I said.

She didn't trust me enough, I thought as I put on my boots at the door. On the bus trip to Toronto, when she'd seemed so excited, it wasn't the cheerleading competition that was on her mind. It wasn't cheerleading at all. It was something else. Something that I was absolutely clueless about.

A secret.

That really hurt.

The next morning, I answered all the same questions at the police station. When I asked them when they were going to start looking for Arielle, they wouldn't give me a straight answer. All they would tell me was that they'd circulated her photo and some details of her disappearance through both police forces. But that was it.

As I was about to leave, the interviewer, an older guy named Detective Fuller, asked me a question no one had asked before. "Did she have a private email address? One her parents might not know about?"

"She had at least three addresses," I told him. "The home one and two others. I don't know them off by heart. But I have them on my computer."

Detective Fuller gave me his card. "Send them to me," he said.

Not even "please" or "thank you," I thought, as I walked out. Just "send them to me," as if I'd give up my best friend's secrets that easily.

But when I thought about the despair I'd seen on Mrs. Kuypers's face, I knew I'd do just that.

chapter sixteen

I turned on the computer as soon as I got home and did a search of my inbox to find Arielle's addresses. There were lots of messages from her home email address. Most recently, there were details about the Toronto trip, most of them sent to the whole team.

I had to look harder to find messages from her other addresses. A note she'd sent me from Toronto when she was checking out residences was sent from her iPhone.

I pasted that address into a message to the detective.

The third address was gesso91@gmail.com. There were only a couple of messages from that one. The most recent was the art portfolio. It was sent to me alone, no other recipients.

I wondered if she'd ever sent that portfolio out, and if so, to whom. I looked through the pictures again. As always, the images sent a chill up my spine. They were pictures that kept secrets.

I sat in my chair for a long time, looking at the carnival picture. There was a title under the picture. *My Girl*.

I went online and and googled *My Girl by Arielle Kuypers*. Arielle had been on the computer a lot recently. I remembered her telling me about the artist who'd admired her work, but I couldn't remember his name. I wasn't expecting to find anything, and I didn't on the first try. But when I tried again, this time using *My Girl* with *gesso91*, I got a hit to a bulletin board. The board was hosted by a site for young artists.

There was a conversation thread about Arielle's painting. Three different people had commented. One was the site moderator. The other two were "Redmeg," a seventeen-year-old girl who, according to her profile, specialized in "fantasy illustration." The other was someone who called himself "TheBeneFactor."

"The BeneFactor." I said it aloud, trying to remember if this was the artist Ari had talked about. I clicked on his profile. A pop-up advised me that TheBeneFactor did not accept unsolicited portfolios. A search on the word *benefactor* turned up too many hits. I was stumped.

I spent another hour on my computer, trying, without success, to figure out the identity of Arielle's friend.

I felt alone in a way I never had before. I knew I ought to be worried about Arielle—and about Liam too—but what I really felt was hurt. Besides my parents, Ari and Liam were the two people I trusted and counted on most in the whole world. Now both of them were gone, and provincials were just four weeks away. I was not only trying to adjust to being a flyer, but I was suddenly the team captain too.

When Arielle made me assistant captain, I thought she'd done it to put an end to Shona's little mutiny. Now I wondered if she'd planned this all along. If she was already preparing to bail out on the team and leave me to pick up the pieces. It was a cruel trick, especially considering I could barely manage my own problems. Now I had twelve other girls to worry about.

chapter seventeen

The next day at school, I made my way down to the art room at lunchtime. I needed to talk to Ms. Currie, the art teacher, to see if she knew anything about someone called The BeneFactor. But how was I going to talk to Ms. Currie without raising her suspicions about Arielle? Ari, of course, was one of Ms. Currie's favorite students. If she thought I knew something about Ari's whereabouts, she'd want me to report it to the police. Even though that seemed like the logical thing to do, Ari had kept me in the dark about her plans because she knew I would blab under pressure.

I needn't have worried. The art room was locked. There are expensive supplies in there. It made sense that Ms. Currie would lock it up when she wasn't there. I let go of the doorknob and turned around to leave. Then I saw the bulletin board display on the wall across from the art room:

A Career in Fine Art—Not Just a Fantasy.

The display was part of a schoolwide career-day project. Many classes and labs had these boards up to highlight the practical applications of the subjects we were learning. I'd contributed a profile of a physiotherapist I'd interviewed to the Health display. I leaned in closer to scan the bulletin board, which housed a collage of art pieces and the careers they reflected. A piece of gift wrap, for example, framed a photo of a person working at a stationery design company. A page of print included a long list of web links, organized into categories. I zeroed in on the list marked *Government grant and other funding support for artists.* I pulled out my iPhone and typed in four URLs from the list. The most promising one was to a website that had information about private donors.

I stuffed my phone back in my purse and walked quickly away from the art room. If I was lucky, there'd be no need to talk to Ms. Currie after all.

After I got home from school, I only had about twenty minutes to go online before cheerleading practice, but it was enough. One of the private donors profiled on the website from the bulletin board was a man named Trey Benedict. The first hit, when I googled the name, was a newspaper review of an art exhibition. According to the reviewer, Trey Benedict's work was "arch." What was arch? Was it good or bad? There was no photo with the article, so I moved on until I found a page about a juried art contest for youth. Trey Benedict was on the three-member jury. I clicked to enlarge his photo. He was a white guy, with a shaved head, thin lips and small features. He stared intently at the camera. It was hard to tell his age. I guessed somewhere in his thirties.

Trey Benedict, the bio said, is a multimedia artist based in Toronto. He is known for his collaborative work, including the creation, with sculptor Cheri Tepperman, of an award-winning permanent installation for the lobby of the prestigious Harwood Club in Oakville. An enthusiastic supporter of young artists, Benedict created the BeneFactor Foundation, which offers exclusive mentorships to emerging young artists.

Exclusive mentorships. I had to find out what that meant. Trey Benedict was based in Toronto. Arielle had disappeared in Toronto. She was with him. I was sure of it.

I was desperate to find out more, but I had to leave for cheerleading. I couldn't afford to be late. I was the captain.

As soon as I'd changed, Coach Saylor took me aside and asked how I was coping. I told her the truth. The idea of being captain of the Starlings completely freaked me out, and I wasn't sure I was up to the task.

She made her *I'm disappointed* face at me. "Well, Marnie," she said, "you're going to have to fake it. These girls need leadership. I can only do so much." She ran a hand through her curly hair. I could see that she was tired. She had been interviewed by the police too. "First of all, you need to tell me whether you want me to replace Arielle."

I opened my mouth, but she interrupted me before I could say anything.

"Not with a new captain. You're stuck with that gig. I mean with a new base."

"I'm the one who has to decide that? Not you?"

She nodded. "Arielle decided to replace Emma with you and to bring Lucy on. It's your call."

I was quiet for a moment, thinking. Our team had been through a lot. I wasn't sure the girls were ready to adjust to a new member. "I'd rather have Barb do it, if she's willing. And use Jada as a spotter when we need one. I'll let the girls know."

Coach nodded.

Having made at least one real decision calmed me down a little. When the warm-up was over, I scooted to the front of the room and did my best to deliver a pep talk.

"Hey," I said. I had to repeat myself a couple of times before the girls quieted down to listen. They weren't used to speeches from me. "We've got some business to discuss. We didn't do too badly at the Great Lakes, considering."

Shona made a face, but she didn't correct me.

"We were in the middle of a crisis, but we got through the routine without any major screwups. We've got provincials coming up, and there's no reason why we're not still in the running."

I looked at Barb. "Barb, I want you to take Arielle's place in stunt team three. When you need a spotter, you'll use Jada. We'll work through the choreography changes today. Are you ready?"

I looked around the room for reactions. Lucy and Priya were smiling at me, but there were a lot of skeptical faces. Shona had her head down, pretending to fiddle with her shoelace. What exactly did she have against me? I was sick of her attitude. It didn't do anything for the team.

"Okay. Places," I said, with as much authority as I could muster. "We're doing 'Groovy.' From the top."

When practice was over, I followed Shona to her end of the locker room. "Can I have your phone number?" I asked her.

"You already have it," she reminded me. "Didn't Arielle send you the contact file when she made you assistant captain?"

"Oh," I said. "Right."

"Why would you need to call me anyway?" she asked.

"Tell you later," I answered.

I'd just remembered something. Shona knew her way around Toronto.

chapter eighteen

As soon as I got home, I got back on the computer. Whatever an "exclusive mentorship" was, it would be hard to argue that Arielle was not worthy of one. I was no judge of art, but I knew Arielle's paintings had earned praise from people who were. She was smart, beautiful and talented, with her life precisely on track. It seemed, now, that those things hadn't mattered much to her. She'd wanted to be an artist more than anything else. And she'd apparently decided that she had to run away to do it. I guess her parents were stricter than I ever realized. I leaned back in my desk chair. I hadn't even figured out where Trey Benedict lived or where his mentorship program was or how it worked. But I knew that Arielle's parents would be grateful for even the little scraps of information that I did have. So why hadn't I called them yet? I probably would have to call the police too. I fished Detective Fuller's business card out of my purse.

Then I put it away again. Wherever Arielle was, she wanted to be there. She'd planned her disappearance with a great deal of care. She'd shipped her paintings. She hadn't told a soul. Not even me. She didn't want to be found. And here I was, trying to help her parents—and the police—find her.

Maybe I owed it to her to find her on my own. She was my best friend. I could find out if she was okay, and then make a decision about who to tell.

There was no address for Trey Benedict on the web. Not surprising. He probably had fans. He might not want them showing up at his door.

There was an address for the BeneFactor Foundation in Richmond Hill, Ontario. Box 2290, Red Maple Road. There was no phone number though, and when I looked up the address on Google Maps, there was a stationery store at that location. So it was a mailing address located in a stationery store, not a real office. That didn't mean anything. Lots of businesses have addresses like that. But it was no help.

If I was going to track down Benedict, I'd have to do it the same way Arielle had. I went to the young artists' bulletin board that I had bookmarked, and hit the button marked Register. I typed in "Flygirl" for a user name, and "Starlings" for my password. Easy as that, I was in.

chapter nineteen

Trey Benedict didn't come online until nearly eleven thirty that night. I knew better than to pounce on him right away. I'd introduced myself to the group when I first joined, and I posted a general question every half hour or so, to make sure my user name popped up on the list now and then. I wanted to look like a legitimate member.

I read all Trey Benedict's posts. Most of the time he was giving advice. He seemed to enjoy the mentor's role. But in a couple of posts, he answered questions about his own work. He was working on some kind of "installation." I wasn't sure what that meant, but I learned that it involved metalwork sculptures. First he had to do drawings of the sculptures though. He promised to post the drawings directly to the board for all to see.

By now, everyone at school seemed to know that Liam and I had broken up. As soon as she found out, Priya had started following me around like I was on suicide watch. "You two were, like, the cutest couple in this school," she moaned. "What happened?"

I shrugged. "Don't ask me," I said. "He didn't explain."

And anyway, I thought, I wasn't sure I even cared. I'd been trying for months to be patient with Liam's new moodiness. I'd done everything I could to prove that I'd stand by him while he got over his depression. It was wrong of him to turn his back on me so completely. Something inside me was shifting. I was going from feeling abandoned to feeling angry.

For the first time in my life, I was on my own. And being mad instead of lonely made it easier to deal.

When I got home from school, I logged onto the artists' site. Nothing yet. Benedict was obviously a night owl.

So I went out for a run. It was March, and we'd had a mild spell. The streets were clear. I ran for only fifteen minutes or so, but it felt good to move. It made me feel competent. In charge. When I got home, I pushed the coffee table aside in the family room and marked out some changes to the choreography for the "Midsummer" routine. With only one tumbler, I needed to find a way to make us look balanced. Pulling out Priya and Ashleigh, the spotters from groups one and three, for some simple tumbling moves during basic stunts would accomplish that. It would provide more visual interest at floor level. Besides, using only two bases for lifts looks less cluttered. It also makes you look cocky, like you don't need spotters.

Priya, I knew, was a decent tumbler, so she'd be able to do it. Ashleigh was more of an unknown quantity. I dialed her number.

"Hi, Mar," she said.

"Hi," I said. "Hope I'm not calling too late. I need to know what kind of tumbling you can do. Can you do a handspring?"

She laughed. "I can do a back tuck, thank you very much. I'm not just a platform for Keri to stand on, you know. What's up?"

"I'm tinkering a little with 'Midsummer.' I want to pull you and Priya out for a couple of tumbling runs."

"Go, girl," Ashleigh said.

"What do you mean?"

"Nothing," she said. "I was worried about you for a while. You seemed pretty shaken up about Arielle. But it sounds like you're on the job now."

I smiled. After Arielle, Ashleigh was the most mature girl on the team. She should have been assistant captain. Her support meant a lot to me. "Thanks," I said.

"Any news about Arielle? The forty-eight hours are up now, right? The police must be searching."

I explained that the search was on hold. Ari was eighteen, she'd shipped her paintings somewhere, and there was nothing to suggest she was in danger. "It's not like she's a missing child," I told Ashleigh, "or even a runaway teen. According to the police, she's an adult. Basically, she's moved out with no forwarding address. Not really a police matter."

"Her parents disagree, I'll bet," said Ashleigh.

"Yep," I said.

It was after midnight. I was exhausted when Benedict finally uploaded his sketches. But I was glad I'd stayed up. When I scrolled down to the second one, a flash of recognition jolted me fully awake. The sketch was of a boy on a skateboard, shoulders hunched, chin tucked down into his collar. Arielle's cousin. *My Girl* was there too. There was no mention in his post of Arielle's name, but Benedict was using Ari's paintings as the basis for his sculptures.

But why would Benedict make pencil sketches of Arielle's paintings? And why had he called them first-draft sketches? And why wasn't he giving Arielle any credit?

It didn't seem wise to ask him those questions directly. Instead, I asked him for an application to his mentorship program. There was a note in his profile that mentioned the BeneFactor Foundation and how it offered "yearlong residential apprenticeships to emerging artists." I also asked where the studio was located. I knew that once I found him, I'd find Arielle.

chapter twenty

When I went online the next morning, a note from Trey Benedict said he was sorry to advise me that there were currently no mentorship openings available. He was grateful for my interest and urged me to post my work to the bulletin board for the group to critique. He didn't answer my question about the studio's location.

I looked at his sketches again. They were in pencil. Some were better than others.

First-draft sketches. Of finished paintings? I don't know much about art, but it didn't make much sense to me.

After cheerleading practice, I approached Shona. "You taking the bus tonight, Shona?"

"Yeah," she answered, sounding suspicious. She hadn't seemed happy, earlier, about my new choreography. I think she preferred me as incompetent as possible.

"Do you have time to grab a coffee with me first?"

She told me she didn't drink coffee. I felt like telling her she could order a tall glass of air, for all I cared. But instead, I said I needed to talk.

We sat down in a diner booth. Shona looked uncomfortable. I wondered if she was expecting me to give her a hard time for trying to undermine me.

"I need your help with something," I said.

She waited.

"You have family in Toronto, right? Or near there?"

"Stouffville," she said, as though every-body knew where that was.

"What about Richmond Hill?" I asked. "Is that near Stouffville?"

"Sorta," she said. "What's this all about?"

"I need to go there," I told her. "Without my parents knowing."

Shona frowned, trying to look like she was deep in serious thought. She still looked like a nine-year-old kid, but I kept that opinion to myself.

"That," she said haughtily, "can be arranged."

I was careful not to laugh. Unbelievable. She was actually going to help me.

"Like, how?" I asked.

"My grandparents are constantly bugging me to visit," she said. "I could call them. And I could say I was bringing a friend along." I must have looked suspicious, because she added, "Duh. I know we're not friends. But we need Arielle back if we're going to win this thing."

Thanks for the vote of confidence, I thought. But what I said was, "Thanks, Shona. It would be a big help. And I'll pay for everything, okay?"

Two hours later, she called me at home to confirm that we were welcome at her grandparents' place for Friday and Saturday night.

"We have cheerleading practice Sunday," I reminded her.

"We'll be back in lots of time," she said.

"Um, okay...," I said.

"And where is it in Richmond Hill that we're supposed to go?" she continued.

"I have no idea," I confessed. "I'm only guessing Benedict lives in Richmond Hill, since his post-office box is there."

She paused before she spoke again. "Didn't you say he's a famous artist? It shouldn't be so hard to find him. We need to call someone who knows about art. Like an art professor or something. You want me to make some calls?"

"No," I said, wishing I'd been the one to think of that. "I'll do it. But Shona..."

"Yeah?"

I hesitated. "That's a really good idea," I admitted. "And it's nice of you to do this for me. This trip."

"You are paying my bus fare, right?" she asked, as if my offer to do so had been her reason for helping me out.

"Of course," I said.

"Then no sweat."

The next morning, I left messages with four different art professors. Only one called back. I was beginning to wonder whether Trey Benedict was famous at all. But Professor Chava Hartz from York University had clearly heard of him.

"He's a sculptor," she confirmed. "But not exclusively. He used to work with textiles. Did you say your art teacher actually assigned you this guy to profile, or that you chose him on your own?"

"Assigned," I lied.

"Oh," she said, sounding surprised. "Well, yes, I'm fairly sure he's still based in Richmond Hill. I have his contact details on file. Email me, and I'll send them to you." She paused, and then she said, "Listen, Miss..."

"Goodwood," I told her. "Marnie Goodwood."

"How old are you, Marnie?"

"Sixteen," I said.

"Uh-huh...well, Marnie, apart from the contact information, I'm not sure I can be of much help in terms of information about Trey Benedict. But let me give you another number to call, okay?"

I took down the number she recited for a guy named Frank Comiskey. "Is he an art professor too?" I asked.

"No," she said. "He's a journalist."

chapter twenty-one

It was 10:00 PM when we reached Shona's grandparents' house. We stayed up for two more hours looking at photos from their recent Australian trip. But when I woke up the next morning at seven, Shona was already out of the shower.

I sat up in my bed. "You really don't need to come with me, Shona."

"You don't know where you're going," she said in a tone that suggested I might even need help finding my way out of bed.

"I printed off some maps," I replied.

"Well, I'm coming," she said. "Get over it."

At breakfast, she told her grandparents we were going to a dancewear store. "You know, Gram. Where I used to get my gymnastics outfits."

"Then we'll drive you, dear! That's such a long way..."

"We already got our bus tickets," Shona lied. "We're all set."

The trip to Richmond Hill took three different buses, with a twenty-minute wait for one of them. If I'd been alone, there would have been plenty of time to get nervous. But with Shona, I felt torn between irritation and fear. Her excitement just made it worse.

"So," she asked, "when we get to the house, are you going to tell him you're Flygirl from that artists' site? Or are you going to say your real name? Because I was thinking, if you were going to say you're Flygirl, I should—"

"I was just going to knock on the door and ask for Ari," I said.

"Oh," she said.

When we got out at the stop nearest Benedict's address, we had to flag down a cab. "We're going to five-eleven Straightarrow Court," I told the cabbie.

The driver studied his GPS screen. "That's gonna be a fifteen- or sixteen-dollar fare," he warned.

"It's okay," Shona told him. "She's paying." She grinned at me and hopped in the cab.

After ten minutes, we entered the fanciest neighborhood I'd ever seen. High stone fences and ironwork gates protected tennis courts, pools and sprawling mansions. The contrast between this place and downtown Toronto was dramatic.

"If Arielle is here," Shona said, "I don't think she's in much danger."

"No," I agreed. Peering through the hedges, I began to wonder how Arielle would react to being found.

"Here we are," the cabbie announced, reaching the end of a long dead-end street. "This the place?"

"Yes, thanks," I said, even though the elegant Japanese-style gate bore no name-plate, and you couldn't see the house beyond. The number was right. We climbed out of the cab.

"Do you want me to wait?" the driver asked.

I looked at Shona, standing awkwardly in the road in her silly pink fur-trimmed parka. I realized how we must look: two teen girls, both tiny for our age, our store-brand clothes betraying our small-town origins. "Nope," I told him, trying to be cool. "Mr. Benedict is expecting us."

I waited until he drove out of sight before pressing the gate buzzer.

"Hello?" a crisp female voice replied.

"Uh...yes," I said. "I'd like to speak with Arielle."

"Who is this, please?" the woman asked. "Is Mr. Benedict expecting you?"

Before I could decide what to say next, Shona piped up. "We're not here for Mr. Benedict. We're friends of Arielle's."

There was a pause and some static, as if the woman had covered the intercom receiver with her hand. Out of the corner of my eye, I saw movement up in a tree. A small, motorized camera lens pivoted slowly toward us.

"I think you must be mistaken," said the woman. "This is the Benedict residence. There is no Arielle here." Then she hung up.

Shona and I looked at each other. "Ring it again," she said.

We tried the buzzer a few more times, but it was clear that we weren't getting in. We heard a crunch of footsteps on gravel. A big man in a skullcap and dark glasses suddenly appeared on the path.

"Hey!" I called out to him. But he just stared menacingly at us, turned around and disappeared in the direction he'd come.

Spooked, I elbowed Shona in the ribs and walked briskly around the corner, forcing her to follow me. I didn't stop until we were fifteen meters from the gate.

"Was that some kind of guard?" she asked, incredulous. "What kind of artist has a bodyguard?"

"And there's a camera too," I said. "For all we know, they can hear us, even without the intercom."

"But we aren't doing anything wrong," she said. "They are. That woman definitely sounded like she was covering something up."

I thought so too, but standing there ringing the bell wasn't doing us any good.

We sat down on the curb to consider our options. A freezing wind kept blowing Shona's fine blond hair into her eyes. She was shivering. She wrapped her arms around her bony gymnast's knees.

"First," I said, "we need another cab." I dialed the number on the card our driver had handed us. Once the cab was on its way, I dug around in my purse for the number the art professor had given me.

"Comiskey," drawled the journalist when he answered. "Like whiskey..."

"Pardon?" I asked.

"Nothing," he said. "Can I help you?"

I explained that Professor Chava Hartz had said he might be able to help us. With information about Trey Benedict.

"I know Benedict," he interrupted. "But who's Hartz?"

"An art professor," I said. "But it doesn't matter. It's Benedict I'm interested in."

"And who are you?" he asked.

"I'm nobody," I said impatiently. "I'm here with a friend from Stratford, Ontario. We're cheerleaders. We're looking for our missing friend."

To my surprise, Frank Comiskey invited us to meet him in Maple. He gave us the address of a coffee shop near his apartment building. I said we'd be there at two, even though I had no idea where the town of Maple was.

chapter twenty-two

Maple ended up being so close that we arrived almost forty-five minutes early. We had to wait forever in that coffee shop. True to my word, I paid for Shona's hot chocolate and bagel.

"Benedict's neighborhood is pretty sweet," I said, trying to make conversation. "I guess he really is a famous artist."

"Famous creep, you mean," Shona said. "Kidnapper. Maybe child molester."

I shook my head. "Arielle's no child. And she wanted to go there. She won some fancy mentorship. You have to apply for it. I tried to apply, and he wouldn't even give me an application form. You have to be really good." I wrapped my hands around my cup to warm them. "I don't know, Shona," I said. "Maybe we shouldn't be here. We could ruin things for her."

"Are you serious?" Shona choked. "He ripped off her paintings! And that woman on the intercom pretended Arielle isn't even there!"

"Maybe she isn't," I said.

"She is."

I stayed quiet for a moment. "Yeah," I said. "I'm pretty sure we're right about this. But she came here out of her own free will. She had her paintings shipped and everything."

"Maybe not," Shona said. "Maybe Benedict did that. Maybe he sent his henchmen to her house to steal them."

I smiled. "I don't think artists have henchmen, Shona."

She looked offended, and I felt a little bad. I was starting to realize that seeming clever and mature was very important to Shona. I guess maybe it's hard to be a four-teen-year-old girl on a team with older girls.

"But you're right," I added to make her feel better. "An ethical artist wouldn't pass someone else's work off as his own, I don't think."

Frank Comiskey took a long look at the two of us when he walked in through the coffee shop doors. He was trying not to laugh.

"What's your problem?" Shona snarled.

He shook his head. "Nothing. Welcome to Maple, undercover cheerleaders."

Comiskey explained that he was a free-lance journalist. He wrote a lot about criminal law: white-collar crime, fraud. "Long trials," he said. "Scandals. If someone rich or famous has done something to embarrass him- or herself, I'm the guy the newspapers call." He gave a tired little half smile that suggested he wasn't entirely proud of the work.

"You don't like doing it?" I asked.

"It depends," he said. "There are some things the public needs to know and other things they don't. You girls want a hot chocolate or something?"

"No, thanks," said Shona. "We want to know about Trey Benedict."

"Well, technically," Comiskey said, "I'm not allowed to report any of this. There's a gag order in place," he explained. "You know what that is?"

"Sort of," Shona said.

"There are charges pending against Mr. Benedict," Comiskey said. "The court has decided that there are matters that, if reported by the media, might unfairly prejudice his case."

"Charges pending?" I asked, really worried now. "Then why isn't he in jail?"

"Whoa, Nelly," said Comiskey. "You only go to jail before trial if you're dangerous."

"He has our friend," Shona blurted out.

Comiskey frowned. "Your friend is an artist?"

We told him about Arielle running away, about the artists' bulletin board and about Benedict claiming her work as his own.

Comiskey nodded. "I've heard this story before. Tried to report it. But it's complicated," he explained. "Benedict alleges—when he's forced to acknowledge the girls' work at all, that is—that these girls are willing collaborators. He's their mentor; the works he produces are artistic collaborations."

"So then why does he need henchmen?" Shona challenged.

"Henchmen?" Comiskey laughed. "I'm guessing you met Eduardo. He's some kind of bodyguard, never leaves Benedict's side. If you ask me, he's just there to make Benedict look important."

I'd been quiet while they talked. It was all coming together in my mind. "He finds talented young artists and he uses them," I interjected. "Because he doesn't have any real talent of his own. He's paranoid someone will find out. It explains the gag order, and the guards..."

Comiskey smiled. "I guess cheerleaders only play dumb."

"We do not!" Shona shot back.

"So," I asked him, "what are the 'matters' you mentioned before? The things that the gag order prevented you from reporting?"

Comiskey shrugged. "Off the record, then. There was a story going around about a boat. A fancy yacht. It belonged to the stepfather of a girl whose family sued Benedict. It sunk one night. The rumor was that Benedict and his friend Eduardo were involved. That it was some kind of threat to the girl's family." He shrugged again. "Far-fetched, in my opinion. If it's any comfort to you," Comiskey continued, "there's never been any suggestion that Benedict's ever hurt an artist. But if this Arielle were my friend, I'd tell her to get out of there."

"But we can't even talk to her," I said.

"If there's anything I can do to help," Comiskey said, "you know where to find me."

After he'd left, Shona and I sat staring at each other.

"You heard what he said," Shona said. "We have to find a way to talk to her. But we'll never get past that gatekeeper."

I nodded. "Then we have to find another way in."

Once we'd worked out a basic plan, Shona called her grandmother. "So roast the chicken anyway, Gram! You and Grandpa still have to eat, right?" She looked at me and rolled her eyes. "No, Greek food is not better than your cooking. But Marnie's never been to Greektown. I promised to show her a good time." Then she turned her back, not wanting me to overhear.

I moved closer.

"Marnie's the new captain, Gram. I don't like her, but I have to suck up to her."

When she hung up, I crossed my arms over my chest and glared at her.

"What?" she challenged. "We have to go back to Benedict's. It has to be after dark.

What was I supposed to say?"

"I don't care what you tell your grand-mother, Shona," I said. "What I'm tired of is the way you act toward me."

"What do you mean?" she asked, as if she didn't know.

"You act like being a cheerleading champion is all you care about, but then you diss me to other people."

She looked confused.

"I'm your team captain, Shona. Like it or not. So how is disrespecting me going to further your goals?" I couldn't believe I'd just said that. Go, Marnie. I waited a long time for her answer.

"I don't know," she whispered, so quietly I could barely hear.

I took a deep breath. "All I'm saying is, you don't have to like me, but you did agree to help me. So how about you drop the diva act and just follow through with what you agreed? I'm grateful that you're here. It would have been much harder to find Arielle without you. Thank you. Now, smarten up."

For once, Shona seemed at a loss for words. She had a funny look on her face, a strange mix of shock, hurt feelings and maybe even a little respect. Before she could say anything to contradict me, I slid my chair out and hopped to my feet. "Let's go. We've got some research to do."

We went from the coffee shop to a library, where we could scope out the Benedict property on an online satellite map.

His lot was at least forty meters wide. There were trees, especially on the west side. It was impossible to tell what kind of fencing surrounded the place.

"It'll be ordinary fencing," Shona guessed. "He's got cameras at the gate, but he's just an artist, after all. It's not, like, a secure compound."

"What makes you think that?"

"Like you said. Arielle wanted to go there. She paid to go there. He's not keeping her there against her will."

I pointed out a shed a third of the way along the west-side fence. "I think we should climb here. Then we can hide between the shed and the fence. But we'll have to go through the neighbor's property to do it."

Shona nodded. "I'm in."

chapter twenty-three

We waited until dark to call the cab, but when we got to the end of Straightarrow Court, there was more light than I'd imagined. Streetlights. Also, many of the trees we'd seen on the satellite image were bare. We looked at each other nervously.

"What exactly do we do," Shona asked, "when we get in?"

I shrugged. On the bus to Richmond Hill the day before, I'd imagined our visit as a rescue. But it isn't a rescue if the person you're rescuing doesn't want to leave. "We'll just talk to her," I said. "Tell her about the sketches."

This seemed good enough for Shona. She kept walking.

We stopped in front of the neighbor's house. There were no cars in the driveway, but that didn't mean much. Mansion dwellers probably parked their cars in garages. We moved on until we were beyond the reach of the streetlights and, hopefully, far enough from the house to avoid triggering any security lights.

The neighbor's fence was low and ornamental, definitely not a security feature. So far, so good.

We concentrated on staying out of the remaining patches of snow and moved quickly toward a little cluster of evergreens. I found myself wishing Shona's parka wasn't pale pink, but we hadn't thought to replace it. We had stopped at a pet store to buy a cheap dog collar and leash. A lost dog was our trespassing excuse.

We stopped between the evergreens and

Benedict's high wooden fence. I could feel the cold creeping up through my boots. We peered at the neighbor's house. There was one light on, toward the back. Nothing to worry about.

We couldn't be sure where the shed was on the other side of the fence.

"Boost me up," Shona said.

I made a basket with my hands and popped her up, just like in cheerleading. I was only expecting her to take a look, but she grabbed the top of the fence and swung over. How was I supposed to follow?

"Shona," I hissed. "Pull on this. Hard." I fed the loop at the end of the leash through the lattice near the top of the fence, then took the collar in my hand.

Shona pulled on her end, and I scampered up the smooth boards like a rock climber. I got a boot over at the top, straddled the fence and swung quietly to the ground. Shona nodded approval, her eyes shining with excitement.

There was junk behind the shed. Lumber, and something that looked like a sailboard. There was enough space to keep us in shadow. We peered at the house.

Light poured from several of the front-facing windows, but our side was mostly dark. There was a screen porch on the back.

The description of the BeneFactor Foundation mentorships had mentioned a "self-contained apartment" for the resident artist. I guessed it would be upstairs.

"Let's go," I said. "Avoid that patch of snow and hunker down between the screened porch and that dark window."

We ran as fast as we could. I expected motion sensors and a security light, but nothing happened. We crouched, panting, our backs against the stonework. When we'd caught our breath, we looked through the screened porch, trying to see the far rear corner. There was a little bit of light there.

We crept carefully around the porch, careful to avoid the noisy gravel at the foundation.

Shona pointed at something on the back wall.

"What?!" I gasped.

"Shh," she said. "It's a dryer vent. That's a laundry room. Won't be anyone in there. We can keep going."

We sidled past the laundry-room window. The last window, at the northwest corner, was the one with the light. But it was above our heads. We were too close to the building to see in.

"You'll have to boost me up again," Shona said.

When I did, she instantly ducked back down, almost knocking me over. She stared at me, wide-eyed with panic.

"He's right there! In the window!"

Terror rooted me to the spot. I remembered Benedict's intense gaze. I desperately wanted to run, but Shona had dropped to her knees, and she had my wrist in a vise-like grip.

"Wait," she whispered. "Hush."

We waited, trembling, for more than a minute. "Did he see you?" I asked.

"I guess not," she breathed. "It's an office. His desk faces out the window.

He was looking at a computer screen..."

I nodded. "Well, at least we know where he is," I said. "Let's go."

We reached the corner of the building. A wide trellis extended from the corner. We had to cross the lawn to get around it. We weren't prepared when we stepped right into a pool of light that came from a pair of French doors.

On the other side of the doors, curled up on a couch, watching television, was Arielle. She saw us right away and jumped to her feet. In three strides, she was at the doors.

"Marnie!" she exclaimed, her voice alarmingly loud. "And Shona...," she added, looking even more surprised. "What are you doing here? Come in."

I was afraid to go in, but we needed her to keep her voice down. We stepped into the warmth of the house.

"Why did you come to this door?" she asked. "Have you met Trey?"

"No," I whispered. "Could you keep your voice down, Ari?"

161

"Why?" she asked. Confusion flickered across her face. "He doesn't know you're here, does he?" she finally said, answering her own question.

"His gatekeeper told us you weren't here," I said. "Earlier, when we tried to get in. And your phone's been off for days."

"I know," she admitted.

"You could have told me about all this," I said. "Why didn't you trust me?"

She didn't answer. "There's no reason you can't be here," she said instead. "You're my guests. Sit."

But we wouldn't.

"Are my parents on their way?" she asked.

"No," Shona said. "They don't know. Yet."

"We wanted to find you first," I added. "See what was going on."

Arielle nodded. "Thanks."

I stood, hyperalert, in the doorway, listening for sounds in the house.

"Why are you so freaked out?" Arielle asked. "I love it here. I'm getting lots of painting done. I'm sorry, Marnie, that I didn't tell you what I was doing. But—"

"He's a criminal!" Shona said.

Arielle frowned. "Hardly."

I heard footsteps.

"He made sketches of your paintings," I said hurriedly. "He posted them online. On that site. Without mentioning you." We had to go. Now. Someone was coming.

Shona heard it too, and she grabbed the door handle. I edged toward the door.

"Arielle?" somebody called.

Shona ran out the door, and I followed. "Call me, Arielle!" I said. "Call!"

Eduardo moved into my line of sight. I turned and ran.

chapter twenty-four

Shona made it all the way around the house, but about four meters from the shed she stopped short.

"Run!" I screamed.

But she was frozen to the spot. A big dark shape was barreling toward her. A dog. A huge one.

"Run, Shona!" I grabbed her sleeve, startling her into action. The dog got hold of the hem of her parka, and she yanked it out of the dog's mouth, stumbling backward.

I dragged her around the side of the shed and tried to boost her over the fence, fending off the dog with my boot. The animal was growling like it wanted to tear us apart. Shona went over the fence headfirst, but at least she was out of the dog's reach. I heard her hit the ground on the other side.

There was no time for the leash trick. I scrambled onto the sailboard, the snap of the dog's powerful jaws ringing in my ears. I punched, blindly, in the animal's direction, and missed. I got one leg over, but when I grabbed the top of the fence to stabilize myself, the dog closed its jaws around my wrist, and pain shot up my arm. I swung my leg forward and booted the dog in the throat, and it let me go. I shifted my weight and fell onto the neighbor's side. Shona pulled me to my feet, and we ran, not stopping until we were around the corner.

We leaned, gasping for breath, against the stone wall that bordered the subdivision. "Taxi," I gasped. "Can you make the call?" I fished in my pocket for the card with the phone number. When I handed it to Shona, she stared down at the cuff of my coat. It was dark with blood.

When we were safely in the cab, Shona reached for my arm. "Let me see." She inspected the puncture below my wrist. "You need to go to an emergency room," she said.

"We can't let your grandparents know," I said. But the hole from the dog's tooth was deep. Germs could live in that kind of wound. My whole hand tingled too, and it was a funny color.

"We're supposed to be out for dinner," Shona reminded me. "They won't expect us home until ten o'clock at least. We've got time." She leaned in toward the driver. "We've changed our minds about where we're going. Do you know the Markham-Stouffville Hospital?"

The cab driver shrugged. "That's maybe twenty-five kilometres. Forty-dollar fare."

"It's okay," Shona told him. "I don't mind. She saved my butt back there."

"Thanks," I said.

Shona just smiled.

At the hospital, the triage nurse wanted to call my parents before I got in to see the doctor. Shona was great then too. She convinced the nurse that getting a phone call from an emergency room late in the evening would freak my mother out.

"She's a two-hour drive away," Shona explained. "What if she panicked and decided to drive out here in the middle of the night?"

When the nurse suggested we call Shona's grandparents, she had a story for that too: they were elderly and frail and terrified of driving at night.

I remembered, with a smile, the photos I'd seen the night before of Shona's grandparents sitting on the roof of a Land Rover in the Australian outback. But I kept my mouth shut. For a fourteen-year-old, Shona was pretty good at thinking on her feet. Having her along on this trip had turned out to be way more helpful than I'd expected.

The next morning when we woke up, Shona took one look at my bandaged wrist and told me she was calling Benedict. She put the phone on speaker and dialed.

"Benedict residence." It was the female voice from the gate intercom.

"Trey Benedict, please. My friend was attacked by—"

"One moment," said the woman.

Benedict picked up immediately. "Moe's up to date on all his shots," he said, without introduction. "I don't know what got into him. He's never shown any aggression before."

Shona snorted in disbelief.

"You were trespassing," Benedict added, but not unpleasantly, as if it were no big deal. "I'd like to give you a copy of his immunization records. To put your mind at ease. And of course, I'll cover the cost of any treatment. Where can I meet you?"

"If you think—," Shona began.

I signaled her to calm down, and I leaned in toward the receiver. "Stouffville," I told him. "Stouffville is best for us. There's a café on the main street..." Stouffville was a small town. I figured he wouldn't dare do anything to us in a restaurant on the main street.

Shona made the call to Coach Saylor in Stratford to ask if our cheerleading practice could be moved from three o'clock to six. She even took responsibility, telling Coach that we'd missed our bus and that it was her fault, not mine. I smiled at her as she hung up the phone.

"We've become quite the team, Squirt," I said.

"Don't call me that," she said. But I could tell she was flattered.

Benedict was at the café when we arrived. He made a big fuss about my arm. He was apologetic and charming. It wasn't so hard to see what Arielle saw in him.

"I've made a vet appointment for Moe," he said. "I need to find out why he would behave that way."

"Oh, there's nothing wrong with Moe," said Shona. "Drop the act."

Benedict looked pained. "You ladies really have it in for me, don't you?"

"You have Arielle," I said.

He sighed, leaning back in his chair. "I don't have Arielle, Miss Goodwood. Arielle has me. I'm her mentor. She's staying with me voluntarily."

"Then why did that woman say she wasn't there?"

Benedict pressed his lips together. "Those were Arielle's instructions. As you might imagine, considering the circumstances of her arrival, she's concerned that her parents might try to force her to go home. If you're her best friend, Miss Goodwood, why didn't you just call ahead?"

I squirmed. "She, uh, has her phone off..." I realized how that sounded.

Like Arielle really didn't consider me a friend at all.

"Ah," said Benedict.

My heart sank. Ari really hadn't wanted me to find her. I looked down at my shoes.

But Shona wasn't ready to give up. "What about the sketches?" she demanded. "Why did you sketch Arielle's paintings and pretend that she had nothing to do with it?"

Benedict laughed. "Oh, boy," he said. "Arielle mentioned that last night after you left." He shook his head, as if remembering an irrational argument, the kind you'd have with a child. "My fault for not explaining to her that you can't just go from paintings to sculptures." He said it as if it was something everybody knew. "I work from line drawings," he continued. "That's what those were. But you're right. I must remember that collaborators need to be given credit, even when I'm just posting my scribbles online."

Shona frowned. "Was it Internet scribbling that got you in trouble the last time?

With the other 'collaborator'? The one whose parents called the police?"

I watched Benedict closely. His expression didn't change, but he stiffened in his seat.

"I'm not sure what you're talking about," he said. "But I'm quite sure it's none of your business." He smiled, but his eyes were fixed intently on Shona. "I should probably remind you that trespassing certainly interests the police."

"I wonder," I said quietly, mustering every ounce of courage that I had, "whether setting a vicious dog on two young girls is the kind of dangerous act that might make a judge rethink a bail order."

Benedict slid his chair back with a squeal. "I don't have to listen to this," he said. "You girls are treading a fine line. Very fine. One little push, and who knows where you'll fall."

"Oh," I said, "don't worry about us. We're cheerleaders. We have very good balance."

chapter twenty-five

"Quite the weekend," Shona said as we packed our bags that afternoon.

"Quite," I agreed. "Shona, do you mind if I sleep on the ride home to Stratford? I'm so tired. We can talk about all this later."

She nodded. "Sure."

"It's not you," I added. "You've been absolutely great. I just don't want to think about all this for a while. All that work, and we're no closer to getting Arielle home..."

Shona nodded, zipping up her bag. "And you might be right about her. Benedict's a scary creep, but Arielle can't see it. Hard to rescue someone who doesn't want your help."

It took Arielle three weeks to get around to it, but she finally phoned me. She called on the night before provincials. Shona and Ashleigh were over at my place. The three of us were watching the DVD from the previous year's competition. We were psyching ourselves up, trying to remind ourselves how close we'd come to winning in the past.

We had been a different team back when Arielle was still captain. But team lineups change all the time in our sport. In any sport. Maybe not always with the kind of trauma that our team had experienced, but teams do change, and they go on. That was what I was thinking about when the phone rang.

"You guys can do it," said Arielle, after I told her we were still heading for the provincials.

"Of course we can," I agreed.

"You sound confident," she said. "That's good."

"I'm captain now," I told her. "It's a job requirement."

"You won't miss me one bit," she said.

I paused. I wasn't sure how I felt about her anymore. "You have been missed, Arielle," I said. "The team misses you. But we had to move on. You didn't leave us much choice."

"I know," she said. "And I'm sorry about my timing. But Benedict told me that if I didn't make up my mind quickly, he'd choose someone else for the mentorship."

"I would have thought if he was so supportive of you, he would've given you more time to make the move." Why would an honest mentor force an A-student to drop out in her final semester of high school? Arielle was not as bright as I'd thought.

"And maybe he would have helped you approach your parents. The way you did it put them through hell," I said.

"They had different plans for me," she said. "I know they're disappointed."

"They had hopes for you," I corrected. "But they never knew your plans."

"Marnie," she said, "why are you being so hard on me?"

It was a good question. I wasn't even sure. So instead of answering, I asked if she'd talked to Frank Comiskey. I'd given the journalist Arielle's number. I thought she might trust his account of the allegations against Benedict more readily than she'd trusted mine.

"Yes," she said.

"And?"

"I'm considering my options."

I sighed. "Well," I said, "I'm here, if you need help moving home. Or with anything else. For what it's worth."

"It's worth a lot, Marnie," she said quietly.

chapter twenty-six

Provincials were in Mississauga, outside Toronto. It was a two-hour drive from Stratford, so I was surprised to see Liam waiting in the parking lot when our bus pulled in.

He was leaning against his old beat-up Buick, his long legs crossed in front of him, his arms crossed over his chest. When I approached, he stood up straight, shifting uncertainly. "Your big day," he said.

"It is," I answered cautiously.

"You didn't think I'd miss it, did you?"

I shrugged. "Hard to know what to think, these days."

He looked at me, his eyes apologizing before his lips did. "You've been through a lot. I'm sorry I made you handle it all alone."

"I made out okay," I said. I looked over my shoulder. A few of the girls were filing into the arena.

"Marnie," he said, "I know I did a terrible thing, leaving you by the side of the road like that."

"I can take care of myself."

"I know," he said. He looked miserable.

"I saw you waiting at that farmhouse," I said. I wasn't ready to forgive him, but I thought it might make him feel better to know I didn't hate him. "Thanks for coming," I added. "We can talk later. Come find me at the lunch break."

He nodded. "Go on in. The troops need their leader. I'll be watching from the front row."

When it was our turn to move into the on-deck room, I gathered the girls around me. "We're a team," I told them. "Not exactly the same team as last year. Probably not the same team as we'll be next year. But we're talented. And we're ready. Right?"

There was a murmur of agreement from the group.

"We're counting on each other. That's fine. But when it really comes down to it, each one of you is here for her own reasons. You each chose this," I told them, looking at each girl in turn. "Nobody else can take it away."

I looked at Shona. "Each one of us worries about making a mistake and letting the others down," I said. "But that's a waste of energy. It's yourself that you need to be accountable to. Do right by you. The rest will take care of itself. I know we can do this. We're ready. So let's get it done!"

Our music began. "If you're listening..." I took a deep breath and ran out onto the mats.

Acknowledgments

Thank you to all the cheerleaders in my past and present: my junior-high and high-school teammates; the lovely Pickering Dolphins Cheerleaders (that's you, Kali!) who cheer on my sons' teams; and especially those wonderful women (and a couple of men) from Critical Manuscript and Goal Girls who have been my own personal cheerleaders for the last five years. You folks make Durham Region the best place in Canada to live the writing life.

Nora Rock is a freelance writer and a college professor. She's an avid fan of hockey and football, both the professional kind and the kind her sons play. Nora played high-school football herself and was a cheerleader for many years. She lives in Ajax, Ontario, with her husband and two sons.

Titles in the Series

orca sports